X

DANCE THE DANCE

By the same author

THE CHAROLLAIS

Dance the Dance

Tom Mac Intyre

FABER AND FABER

London

First published in 1970
by Faber and Faber Limited
24 Russell Square London WC1
Printed in Great Britain by
Latimer Trend & Co Ltd Plymouth
All rights reserved

ISBN 0 571 09323 x

For My Parents

Acknowledgements

These stories have appeared in the following:
*Arena, New Irish Writing, The Dubliner,
The Holy Door, The Kilkenny Magazine,
Threshold, University Review, Michigan
Quarterly Review, Short-Story International,
Transatlantic Review*, and *Winter's Tales*.
The stories *Fable*, and *Exposure*, have been
broadcast by *Radio-Telefís Eireann*.

Contents

'You've sung the song, you call that doing,
You've sung the song, then dance the dance.'

ALEXANDER KUPRIN
'The Song and The Dance'

Stallions

One afternoon the housekeeper pounced—

'You're going to the creamery'—the can pushed at me—
'two shillings worth of cream and hurry back.'

She slapped shut the door.

I went down the avenue and on to the road where tar oozed
and gleamed after hours of sun. It was four o'clock. It was
May.

The town lay a good shout off, the creamery half a mile beyond. I set out, past Jack Traynor's who had been a schoolmaster, was now old, and came abroad only to walk in the
downpour; past Miss Farnan's who snatched kindling from
behind hedges and had seen The Blessed Virgin; past Tom
Millar's who housed a motor-bike and greyhounds but was
Protestant. I stopped at Carroll's archway, that day a funnel
of shadows. My eyes pricked. Among the shadows, sloping
round the curve which hid the gap of the other end, was
Albert McElwaine.

There was something up in Carroll's yard.

McElwaine was about my age, his curiosity mine. The cut
of him lured me, the lie of his back, the drag of his hand as he
took the bend—blurring himself to the wall. I followed,
hastening through, round the blind curve and into the yard, a
square, which held the light like a bowl.

Ten or twenty men were standing about, talking in groups,
smoking, testing the ground with ashplants or nubbly black-

thorns. A line of carts to one side, cherry and blue, shafts down, backsides up, harness slack in their bellies, had gone to sleep. There was a green whiff of droppings, and the stomping and tossing of horses fidgety in the dark stables. Nothing was happening. McElwaine, by himself in a far corner, hadn't seen me yet.

The creamery?—should I go on?—full of ramshackle noises, floodwaters, pipes which sang and sneezed, churns with portholes and hatches, ladders, platforms, ramps, and a gloom of ice and snow where they stored the butter. . . Maybe I should go on?

From behind the row of carts, someone brought out a black mare, shivery patches of sweat slick on her rump. In the middle of the yard they stopped, waiting, the middle their own. The space had grown while they moved into it. The mare jibbed and wheeled.

I stole to the edge of the ashplant and blackthorn ring.

As if a thousand locks had snapped, a door to the left flew open. A stallion ricochetted into the sun, pawed for the sky, and let out a whinny that flared over the town.

Dread turned inside me. Between those great open haunches guilt swayed.

Chestnut against the whitewash walls he rose again, fetlock to crest shining like fire and, twenty feet up, two polished hooves flailing my body with velvet blows.

Excited and glancing, the mare waited. For the first time, I saw the ostler, puny, and the reins. Flanks in a quiver, the stallion broke forward, closed, reared and plunged. Guiding in the reek and sweat flashed the red hand of the ostler. The stallion, straddled, pumped like his taut hamstrings must split. Then the ostler again, parting them, the spill passed on. The mare was led away. Snorting and champing, the chestnut was stalled.

Against the butt of a hobnailed boot, a farmer near me
rapped his pipe—

'Well, boy, what d'ye make of it?'

He grinned down over a porter belly.

Flushed and floundering, I left. I was smeared—at the
same time dazed by the pounding of velvet hooves.

Every Monday I escaped to the yard. McElwaine was always
there. And a few others I knew in school. Here we never spoke.
Singly, privately, we awaited each loud unbolting and the rush
that followed. It was like watching the start of the world.

Curried and ribboned and bobbed, the stallion roiled my
dreams.

At home no one noticed.

I saw the future: fifty-two Mondays bright and luscious in
the year.

On my fourth visit, Lil Carroll, ladling sugar into two-
pound bags, looked out a spidery window, saw me criminal
among the men. And told.

When Mother called I was eating in the kitchen.

'Come up here you.'

Fearful, I rose and followed her up to the parlour.

First she stood with her back to me, staring out on the
flower-garden, said nothing. Then she turned, making a slow
sign of the cross, and met me with a dead face.

'Where were you this afternoon?'

'Playing football.'

'Football!' she mocked. 'In Carroll's yard?'

I eyed the garden behind her.

'May,' she said, 'Our Lady's Month.'

I shrank to a culprit.

'If I ever hear of you being there again, you'll get a dose you
won't forget.'

I said nothing.

'Promise,' she commanded, 'Come on.'

'I promise'—

Too fast.

There was a pause while she studied me, a long one, and with it I could feel driving between us the fury of the yard, the glare and the ripeness, the sling of that door's opening, the stallion loosed again.

'Go back to your tea.'

I left the room.

'Stallions,' I heard her say on my way down the hall.

Such a Favour

Soon as I got home from school the first thing my mother said was—'How's that ear?'

'Grand.'

I hung up the schoolbag. The year past had been troublesome for the ear: hospital, surgery, drops, powders, and ointments. It seemed to have cleared up altogether now. No mention of it for a month or maybe six weeks.

'It's grand,' I said.

The question was still there. I turned. Freshly, strangely, she was looking at me. 'I want you,' she said, 'to go across to Doctor Harding's and have him check it.'

'All right.'

'And today—be sure.' After which, mind hurrying, she added, 'Now.'

'Right.'

I didn't care. Now or later. She saw me off—her touch light on my shoulder as I went out the door. And from a window of the living-room watched me go down the avenue. Her owning glance. It might have been my birthday. Funny.

Doctor Harding's house below The Model Hill was a sober barracks where everything shone darkly. The doctor, a small man—spruce to his toes, shone too, darkly. In the surgery at the back, instruments flickered, black potions gave a syrupy tang to the close air, and on one of the walls hung half-a-dozen drawings of a woman's head. The doctor's wife. Of course he's brilliant, people said, an artist, you know, in his way.

'Well, child?' He took the lobe of my ear between finger and thumb, put me sitting down, 'How is it?'

'Fine, Doctor.'

The pair of white hands angled me. A mirror-gadget tied to his forehead collected light from a lamp and fed it into my ear. Inside my skull, a faint warmth flitted. He examined, poked, probed, while I winced from the pliable needles by which he lived.

'Any pain?'

'No pain.'

He poked some more, dazed me by washing—the syringe spouted thunder, and then said I could go.

'Never saw it better. Good-bye.' He straightened the door-mat with the polished toe of his shoe as he waved me off, 'Good-bye. Never better. Good-bye.'

'Thank you, Doctor. Good-bye, Doctor.'

For an hour or two I rambled the town, played with the gang. Arrived home, I was instantly summoned. My mother waited in the living-room, a hand on the marble of the mantel-piece. Outside, the crows' grey chatter raked light from the afternoon. And a shower lay in the tops of the beeches.

'Well?'

Her serious face. You have a pious face, ma'am, the butcher said to her on Saturdays, a holy face. Half-joking, whole in earnest. A line went up from the nose, dividing her forehead neatly. Now her curiosity wrinkled into that line.

'It's grand.'

I was hungry for tea.

'Tell me what he said,' she instructed. 'Exactly what he said.'

'That it was grand.' What he'd said exactly, I couldn't remember but—'Just it was grand.'

'You've forgotten,' she accused.

I fumbled. What odds was it? Exactly what he said. I didn't know. The lips, shut, condemned, then pulled it from me— ' "Never saw it better," that's what he said.'

Her face relaxed, expectant.

The clock on the mantelpiece roared something had happened. She looked out the window, back to me.

'You're certain he said that?'

I nodded. Plain as porcupine, I'd heard him. The big room, grey and still a moment ago, was on the move.

'You know whose Feast-Day it is?'

I didn't.

'Blessed Oliver's,' she said, and sat down. Her eyes were wet, bright. She blessed herself, looking at the small fire, and smiled—smile of hers that was open and secret. Suddenly, *Blessed Oliver*, her excitement was in me, and a holy lightness. I flushed—

'You mean'—

The pride of it shocked us, I went from giant to midget and back again, lost myself, found myself, would have held her hand . . . 'The Novena,' she was saying, 'I made The Novena.'

She motioned me to kneel. Astonished, I did, and together we prayed. My ear was a litany, a hymn, the wing of an angel. Through the house Blessed Oliver strode. *Oh, God, who through the labours of Blessed Oliver Plunkett* we prayed, eyes out on sticks we prayed . . . .

I knew all about Blessed Oliver from the history books, and I could remember, besides, lots of evenings.

'Say that prayer now. Until we see how well you know it.'

On a chair before the fire, dragging the hearthrug with my shoes. A visitor there, Mrs. Keegan, who often was. Spoke and looked like a turkey-cock but she was all right. Every day of her life she made a Holy Hour.

'Don't you know the prayer?'—Mrs. Keegan.

My mother—'Stand over there across the room, and give it out for us. Go on.'

Both knitting, glancing up occasionally to encourage me towards an answer. Sliding off the chair, over to one of the windows, standing by the drawn curtains. The wind breaking its neck outside, pelting to get ahead of the rain. Beginning—

'Oh, God, who through'—

'Hands joined.'

Hands joined.

'Oh, God, who through the labours of Blessed Oliver Plunkett, thy martyr and bishop, didst preserve the Irish people in the Catholic faith, grant through his intercession, abundant favours and graces, that he may soon be glorified by thy Church with the honour of canonization, through Christ, Our Lord, Amen.'

Standing there. With my recitation.

'A credit,'—Mrs. Keegan—'Has it like a song.'

'Not so bad'—my mother.

Back to the fire, sitting between them, ready, tasting the mood.

'Blessed Oliver,' Mrs. Keegan, sadly.

Soot falling in the chimney, gouting black fire.

'At Tyburn,' from my mother, and after her pause, 'A dreadful thing.'

Ahead of the rain at last, the wind ferocious outside, the wooden shutters alive, and the iron weights as the windows rattle.

'God grant,' Mrs. Keegan counting her stitches, 'God grant the miracles.'

'God grant them.'

Myself pulled into the chant—'God grant them'—and then, confused, Mrs. Keegan looking at me suspiciously—

'Say the prayer and he'll be canonized. The Lord works through prayer. Isn't that right?'

'Yes'—

Back to the knitting. The fire, slacked earlier by my father, opening small gaps to show the furnace inside. The wind. The wind blowing Blessed Oliver's head down a street from Tyburn, bumping it horribly until a nun or a priest swoops, hides it in black folds—the spitting mob pass—brings it away to Drogheda. Still there, on display. My mother had knelt before the glass case in the side-chapel—

'Unrecognizable—but after all this time what could you expect?'

Murdered by the English. Hanged, drawn, and quartered. Horrible. Still, some day he'd be a saint.

'Two major miracles,' my mother speaking after a while, 'Would do it.'

'Two majors. Prayer will get them. His Divine words—not mine.'

Above the needles, my mother's face tight. That for a time and then, fingers easing, needles gliding into each other, her look opening and an aspiration crossing her lips, *Sacred Heart of Jesus, grant it.*

The English, oh, a dirty crew. Tyburn, a dreadful thing.

'You'll mention it to no one,' I was warned, 'Not a living soul.'

I nodded my word on this. For the time being, anyway, I wanted the news to myself. Tea was ready. At the table and over scrambled eggs, I glowed the singularity of this new thing, fingered the extraordinary ahead. It would be in the papers eventually, I speculated, a photograph, a full description, the evidence. I would be brought to Drogheda, maybe even to Rome. The celebrations when they canonized him—

there would be a day! I could see myself, heady, among pillars and domes, I was being led forward by a robed Bishop, my mother on his other arm, the white figure of The Pope was coming to meet us, the bald head and the glasses smiling. Between The Pope and us on a table but curtained in cloth-of-gold was the glass case from Drogheda, with the head, a choir was singing to deafen you, and—

'What's up with you,' the housekeeper rapped, bringing in the teapot, 'all of a sudden?'

Nibbling brown bread, I hid from her. When she heard she'd have less guff. She went back to the kitchen, and I felt for the chosen ear, the right it was, and scarred. Rain was coming on but the evening fought it. Past the chapel and beyond the lake, my miracle coursed the Tyburn sky.

Next day was Saturday, no school, and I stayed clear of the gang. My mother was busy all day. She visited the Parish Priest, she visited the doctor, she spoke with Mrs. Keegan, and that evening after tea settled herself at the living-room table. Before her was sheaf of notepaper, a list of instructions she'd got from the priest, a note from the doctor, and the address of The Blessed Oliver Plunkett Canonization Association in Drogheda. She wrote while I watched from the fire.

'Is there—a lot of documents?' I asked.

'They have to be copied, and copied'—she finished a page —'and copied.'

When my father came in she never looked up. He sat down by the fire, inspected each of us, sighed.

'It's a wonder you wouldn't have wit, woman?'

'We'll see,' said my mother, 'who has the wit.'

She wrote on. He looked at me, about to say more despite the enmity in my face but my mother interrupted—

'I made The Novena. And you heard what the doctor said.'

Covered sheets of notepaper gathering about her.

'Aye,' my father said, getting up, 'Geraldus Cambrensis, I declare to God, isn't in it with you.'

By Sunday evening the documents were ready, signed and sealed, and on Monday morning they were posted.

'Remember—not a word to anyone for the time being,' my mother had repeated, but Wednesday afternoon during geography class I decided it was only fair my closest friend, Colm Skelly, should know. There was something wrong about sitting there beside him after what happened, and not telling.

'The Meuse, The Mass . . . The Scheldt . . .' said Master Kiernan, 'Examine the Lowlands, boys, examine the Lowlands, and ask . . .'

'I've a thing to tell you,' I said to Skelly. He was drawing goalposts on a picture of Antwerp.

'What?'

One brown eye of his bigger than the other.

'My ear was cured'—I had to force the words through my own wonder—'by a miracle.'

The small eye narrowed.

'Amsterdam for diamonds. If you decide to become a diamond smuggler, you will inevitably spend much of your time in Amsterdam. The Hague . . .'

'Who? What miracle?'

'Blessed Oliver Plunkett.'

'But how do you know, a miracle?'

'The documents,' I told him, 'went off, Monday.'

'What documents?'

His big eye growing.

'To prove it,' I said.

'And you all know the story of the boy who, to save his country from the floods, placed his finger . . .'

Skelly surrendered. He knew when I was lying and when I wasn't. We began to grapple with the details.

'What's the whispers about?'

Jam-Bun Cooney tuned in.

'It's a secret,' I snapped.

I wanted *one* to know but—

'Tell us, Skelly,' said Jam-Bun, 'Come on . . .'

'Think of the boy's swollen finger, the courage of that boy, the threat of the waters . . .'

'I'd rather,' Skelly swore, 'have my right arm cut off nor tell.'

Later that evening my mother announced there'd been a note from Drogheda. The documents had arrived and would be examined. We would be advised in due course.

'What's in due course?' I asked.

'It means "soon".'

Which was fine.

Two days afterwards the bottom fell out of the sky.

'Holy Joe,' said Jam-Bun Cooney in a corner of the school yard at the eleven o'clock break, and let me stare him.

'Which ear?' said Jam-Bun.

Skelly, the bastard, I thought. I turned my back on Cooney and faced Gunn, Murtagh, three or four more, all wearing Jam-Bun's grin.

'Give us your blessing,' said Murtagh, 'Will you?'

The bunch tittered.

'The Miracle-Man,' said Jam-Bun and the other noises and activity of the yard dropping away from us, they took it up, 'Give us your blessing, Miracle-Man, on your knees for the Miracle-Man, Miracle-Man, Miracle-Man . . .'

Dancing they drummed it at me. I had the feeling I was being again and again dipped in one of the big vats of skim-

milk the creamery had, the top all curdled globs and scum-
bubbles that smelled of the pigs who drink the stuff in the
end, dancing they drummed, up and down up and down
holy Joe show us your toe take off your ear and climb on a
pier my miracle nothing in the bottom of the vat until I got
back the energy to run smash through the ring of them race
the yard and make the classroom where I waited trembling
until the bell went and the school filled up again.

'Your own fault—for opening your mouth,' my mother
said.

Next day in school wasn't as bad, but bad enough and that
night, the taste in my mouth sliding into me like poison,
I discovered what they'd done—found out from myself in
spite of myself because the discovery was a sickener all right.
Suppose, I thought, for the first time, suppose it wasn't a
miracle? I slept with the poison, and woke with it. Funnily,
as the attack slackened in school (they tired, not altogether,
but were content with a jeer a day at most), it ran all the more
in me: Suppose it wasn't?

'What are you sulking about?'

She.

'Nothing.'

'Nothing?'

I couldn't keep it in.

'Was there word?'

'No word. You're in a great hurry?'

A month went by. No word. Six weeks. I sulked and blamed
without saying it out: *you got me into this.* I wanted to know,
was it or wasn't it a miracle? Proof. I wanted Rome, and a
choir splitting the roof. I wanted an answer for *them*, the
jackdaws always perched on the school wall—watching me,
no one else—to squawk their gibes. Sometimes they let on to
forget but they never forgot . . .

'The pair of you,' my father said one evening, 'have that child astray in the head.'

'Was there word?'

No word.

'Don't take on to rush The Lord,' Mrs. Keegan warned, 'He's in no hurry.'

And, 'Me Granny's ailing,' said Jam-Bun, 'Could you give us a cure for galloping arthritis?'

Two months passed, and a letter arrived. The documents had been sent to Rome where evidence was being collected. But nothing definite, of course, would be known on the matter for a long time, perhaps even years. . .

I knew they were worried also, uncertain even, only somehow or other they could talk themselves out of it. Bitterly I found my way to recklessness, steadied myself, and spoke. Nobody had been saying much this particular evening which didn't help. I waited for the clock to ring ten o'clock which it did, noisily, and out of the chimes I came with it—

'Suppose it—wasn't a miracle?'

They looked at me.

'Suppose'—

But under the horror in their faces I broke, wept. They gave me three minutes silence. After which Mrs. Keegan, her nose blue, said it would fit me better to be on my knees, thanking Blessed Oliver for a favour bestowed instead of evening my wit to workhouse brats who hadn't been washed since the day they saw the font.

'Go up to bed,' my mother ordered, 'You might have more manners in the morning.'

'And,' she called after me, 'Make an Act of Contrition for that outburst, if you take my advice.'

I had a bad night but awoke with a plan.

'Could we go to Drogheda?' I asked, 'To the Shrine?'

'Why?' My mother studied me.

'I want to. That's all.'

She wasn't impressed.

Mrs. Keegan heard the proposal.

'The Holy Ghost,' she said, knitting-needles flashing, 'works in strange ways.' She stopped to look accusingly at me, 'It wouldn't surprise me,' she added, 'If you received a *sign*. It often happens. Isn't there a Saturday bus?'

Mrs. Keegan's brains, I decided, were in her head and not anywhere else. Because what I was looking for was a sign, a miracle to clinch the miracle. Something past dispute that would shut Skelly and Cooney and the rest of them up for good. Blessed Oliver's voice or a fierce light or—Anything— A clincher.

'All right,' my mother consented, 'Saturday week we'll go.'

That night we prayed gay prayers, and, by the time I walked to the bus with her, Rome was in sight once more, great ceilings, hymns, incense, photographs. . .

'Say the prayer now,' she instructed as the bus started off, 'for our Intention.'

Below breath, we said it together.

Drogheda was hilly streets and the river and traffic thick in the sun. I'd been to Confession and Communion, I was in the State of Grace, I was ready for anything. Please, Blessed Oliver, please. Don't let me down now, don't, please. We went straight to the Church, and up the steps—my feet hardly touching the flight of them—hand in hand. My man inside, waiting. Like meeting an uncle, it seemed, who's been sending you presents from abroad but whom you've never seen. Everything

fizzing inside me. The porch. She stopped to straighten my tie,
fix my jacket. Blessing ourselves, we went in.

The Church was huge, empty or nearly, and silent except
for someone's shoe hitting a kneeler maybe, the noise flying
up and around pillars and shaking the coloured windows
before sliding away into some crack in the stone floor.

'Come on.'

I followed her up the aisle, thinking for a second on the
special way she walked in church, proud, owning the place.
I followed, genuflecting with her towards the altar miles away
as we moved from aisle to aisle—we'd never get to The
Shrine—but eventually she said, 'Here . . . Kneel down . . .'

The Shrine. *Please, Blessed Oliver.*

Candles, flowers, and a big framed picture of him looking
down at me. Severe but I liked the look of him. The glass case.
First I couldn't see it at all, my eyes running too many places
for it, then, following her eyes, I found it.

'Say the prayer.'

I tried to but I'd forgotten the prayer, couldn't find the
start of it. The glass case. And the head. Where was the head
—that wasn't the . . .

Please, Blessed Oliver, I looked up at the picture, please.
Tight, knotting a little, I kept my eyes there. My mother
praying, watching it. The head.

Please, Blessed Oliver. A sign. Something. Now. But the
picture, grey, frowning, Archbishop of Armagh and Primate
of All Ireland said, Look down, down . . . The glass case. I
had to. My eyes cut the gloom of the high window and this
corner and reached it again. That wasn't the head . . . My
eyes stuck. Black as pitch and the size of a handball. Withered.
Sticky. Looking straight at me. Suddenly I was babbling . . .
Oh, God who . . . The head fixed me and wouldn't let go.
Rolling down a street from Tyburn please Blessed Oliver my

hands sweating and my body it looking straight at me thank you God for the glass case anyway imagine having that in your hands the feel of it don't Blessed Oliver don't I want to—

'What's wrong with you? Are you sick?'

I was outside, sitting on one of the steps, wanting to throw up and not able. She was beside me. I nodded, white, looking down the street.

'The bus, was it?'

I shook my head, not looking at her.

'And what then?'

She moved lower to see me properly.

'I want to go home.'

Her face set against me. She knew: *it*.

'You mean you won't go back in and pray—after coming half the country to The Shrine?'

Standing over me. Some people passing on the steps.

'Is he all right, ma'am?'

Man's voice.

'Just an upset. He's all right now.'

Set against me.

'Well?'

Sweat running off me.

'I want to go home.'

We had a cup of tea in a restaurant, and took an early bus home. She never spoke on the way. Coming every so often, between us on the seat, sitting on her gloves, on her bag, the head. Like a charred potato from the back of the oven only something live inside it. Earless but listening to our hard silence.

The Great Sword

Where Syl Jameson came from, no man knew: where bound for was revealed to me alone.

Jesus Christ on a motor-bike, Tom Long, the ganger, named him when he arrived that Friday morning and was taken on in Cranston's Garage. No other way of describing Syl with the long blonde hair flying, bulbed forehead, blazing eyes, and bony narrowing cheeks, mouth, jaw—tearing up the street on a broken-winded autocycle, heading for some job that must be done or the world was at an end.

That was an arrival. About ten o'clock, the sun eating its way up the steely June sky, he soared out of himself.

'Lazarus, come forth,' Mick Carson bawled as Syl was passing.

Mick's pin-head sticking up from a trench in Wolfe Tone Street, where he and a few more were fixing a leak in the main.

The men laughed. About thirty yards up, Syl wheeled and came back, cruising, the autocycle whining and sputtering. And for ten minutes he cruised up and down while Mick and the gang sank lower and lower into the trench, and bullets from Syl's blazing eyes rang above their heads. Eventually, the machine slowing almost to a stop, Syl cried out, over the sputtering engine, over the trench, over the opening windows and the opening doors, cried out in his northern accent—'Woe to the mockers'—the men flattened—'for their eyes are needles. But the eye of a needle awaits them—at The Gate'—

the engine revved suddenly and hummed low again—'The Gate through which they shall not pass.' The engine revived, maintained power, and this time bore Syl away.

'Is he a Protestant?' my Mother asked, 'Or what?'

He was religion-mad—a story flew—had been through, *seen* through, The Church of Ireland, The Presbyterians, The Methodists, The Lutherans, The Witnesses, and The Salvation Army.

At noon I was in Cranston's Garage, that draughty shambles. Storm or calm, the wooden walls rippled and whinged. Only the banked odour of oil and grease supported the roof. Light, soon as it entered the place, fell down and died among the rusting machine-parts which grew from the dirt floor. Albert Cranston met me.

'You're not the first,' Albert said, flinging a spanner aside— rattling a wall from end to end, 'Go on home. He's gone to his grub.'

Albert. A long October briar, his face a berry that would never ripen.

'Stay clear of him,' Albert warned, 'He's trapped lightning, boy, that's what he is.'

He went down the garage, and dropped, groaning, into a pit.

Two o'clock or half past, and Syl was news again.

'You've great hands on you,' Father John Donegan said to him.

Syl had just finished a tricky piece of work on the engine of the priest's car.

'A great pair of hands.'

Rubbing his hands with a rag, Syl stared him.

'All things are possible,' said Syl, 'Don't you know that yourself?' He lowered the bonnet, tightened it. A gay secret ran out of the corners of his eyes and down over his face.

It was Syl's expression, Albert said, upset the priest.

'*All* things?'

'All things,' said Syl, 'All things, that's right—all.'

'I see,' Father John, shoulders chuckling—that was his danger sign, came back, 'Then I suppose that if '—

"Take the word, take that word "all".' Syl's jaw stuck out. And his right hand. Father John looked at it. Scarred. Colour of grease and oil.

'No, go on'—more friendly—'Take it, take it.'

Doubtful, Father John—nod of his head—took the word.

'Right,' Syl went on, 'Right. Now—try and surround it.'

Father John scowled.

'Try it,' Syl leaning against the priest's car, smiles up and down his face jigging encouragement, 'Go on. Try and surround that word "all". Go on, try it.'

So, Father John, nettly, took on to surround the word, ('Good, good, give it the try', Syl kept shoving in), circling it, and squaring it, and God knows what until he was light in the head. He huffed then, and tried to barge his way out by saying that, whether you could or you couldn't, it didn't follow this and you couldn't claim that and in any case—

'Have you it surrounded yet?' says Syl, on hunkers now, very patient, watching the floor.

Father John, ears turning white, started another palaver about logically speaking, and as far as he was taught—

'Have you it surrounded yet?'

Knotting his mouth, Father John glared across at Albert.

'The wee word,' says Syl, laughing to himself, 'the wee word "all".'

Poor Albert paralysed, not knowing whether he was the middle of the week or maybe the end of it.

'I'm not used,' Father John takes out the big stick, 'to being spoken to in—'

'You haven't surrounded it,' Syl rose like a salmon, and lit on him, 'And you won't, and will I tell you why?'

Shouting, quivery with joy. Father John moved back—

'Because it's limitless, man,' says Syl, arms wide, including Albert, including everybody, 'There's no bound to it, none, my God, when you think what's possible'—Albert thought Syl would go up in flames but instead he held out his hand, the hand trembled, and the three of them stared at his palm—'Nothing's impossible once you get inside that—spaceship,' the hand bobbed gently, they all stared again, 'Look at it, will you,' Syl sang, 'and look at it well because there, I'm telling you, is my spaceship'—his voice dropped to a faraway croon that gurgled down to his toes—'the wee, lovely, limitless word—"all".'

He floated out on to the street. The autocycle crackled. They heard him whine down the road.

Everyone had it in half-an-hour, and the procession started to Cranston's. But Syl couldn't be found.

'Out on jobs,' Albert said, and no more.

The afternoon sizzled. At four o'clock he cleared the congregation, twenty of us, idlers, chancers, gawky roamers. We stood outside awhile, and the rumour was that Syl had gone and joined The Dippers—a noisy sect in which, we understood, every man was his own Bishop—and was, at this moment, addressing them in the Meeting-House on Carrickgorman Hill. The Dummy Rogers said No he was fixing a churn in the Creamery. Vinny Gunn said he was in the Barracks on a charge of disturbing the peace.

They were all wrong. He was in our kitchen repairing the electric pump which had bested my Father, Albert, and a dozen handymen over the previous three weeks. I was home at half-four, and found him there. The housekeeper had let him in, and then fled to an upstairs room.

35

'You're—a Collins man,' said Syl when I walked in, and met my unbelievable luck. He glanced at the picture of General Michael Collins, green-and-gold against a background of cloud blue, Commander-in-Chief, National Army, which hung on the wall beside the window.

I told him Yes, I was a Collins man.

Crouched in the corner beside the sink, hands weaving over the pump, he smiled, and asked me what I thought of Collins.

'He was—a great one, Syl.'

Soundlessly, I settled on a chair.

'The greatest,' he corrected, 'the greatest ever lived.'

We looked at each other. We looked at the Collins picture. And there in the kitchen that smelled of turf kept in a tea-chest, and dishcloths the housekeeper had boiling on the stove, Syl opened for me his bag of dreams.

All things were possible, he said. He himself had heard, for example, The Voice Within and The Voice Beyond. He explained how he had heard them, what they had said, and 'the meaning thereof.' He led me into The Cycle of Numbers —seven was his number, and he'd been born under The Sign of the Lion. Truth was The Ocean, Syl told me—'I can prove it.' He did, and then, closing his eyes, went on to demonstrate The Link between all things. Gob open wide as the mouth of The Shannon, I sat on the edge of my arse, hypnotised— but he hadn't even begun. He laid bare The Compass of The Pyramids, and The Greater Compass buried beneath the floors of The Amazon Jungle, unravelled The Black Art and The White, indicated what might be taken from The Koran and what discarded, described how Time opens and Time shuts, gave me the secret of Dominion over The Elements, and The Rule of Animals, quoted Scripture, quoted poetry, quoted the Three Lost Prophecies of Malachy The Thin, and —the sun reaching down to stack the kitchen with spears of

gold, a glister of sweat sitting like chain-mail on his forehead
—asked me if I knew he'd held The Great Sword in his
hand.

'No, Syl,' I whispered.

'I stood alone on the ridge of the world,' said Syl, looking
past me—through the door that let into the hall, 'and I held
The Great Sword of Light, not by the blade either—any eejut
could do that—but by the handle, boy, the handle.'

His hands clenched. And bronze ran in the whites of his
eyes.

It was a blinding flame, he said, that scorched the hearts of
the unworthy but he had looked at it and into it without harm.

'He knew all that,' suddenly he switched—the Collins
picture, 'He held The Great Sword.'

Anger skewered Syl's face.

'Which was why,' he added, 'they struck him down.'

From my chair by the door, I nodded. And waited for what
he would now say. He was coming to something very im-
portant. The sunlight had stopped moving, the spears. Syl's
eyes swung to the edge of his forehead, lay there, glinting,
flickered round corners, flew back to their burning nests.

'There'll be another Great One soon,' he said, 'Another
—Coming. Did you know that?'

Lungs daring me to breathe, I shook my head.

'Well, there will'—again his eyes swung and glinted and
flickered round corners and came home, pleased—'This
could be a great wee country,' he said, 'if it was One, if it
was made whole.'

My lips fluttered.

'Another Great One,' said Syl, 'It's written.'

'Who, Syl?' I asked, 'Who'll it be?'

He examined me. Alight. Circles formed about his mouth,
smiles, tipping nose and chin as they began to move. He

37

seemed perched—on air, God, I thought, don't let him float away on me, don't please. The circles were spreading, the ripple of smiles, Syl bobbing, 'Who, Syl?' I swayed a dry tongue, 'Who'll it be?' He opened his mouth to answer, and the housekeeper—curse her—clattered something upstairs. Straightaway he was on his feet, that was it, gathering wrenches and spanner and washers and grommets and oilrags. He clicked a lever. The pump buzzed and burred, and burred steadily.

'Good luck, boy.'

He was at the door.

'Good-bye, Syl,' I said—flustered.

But I was right. I never saw him again. He didn't even report back to Cranston's. Down the avenue with him, and instead of turning right towards the town, he turned left. The main road north. Forty miles off was The Border. The hedge hid him now. I listened. Somewhere inside the racket of the autocycle bugles began to twirl and spit, and a black cackle of rooks rose. In awe I watched, and Syl swept into sight on Hourican's Brae, wheels flaking on the rise. I watched him grow as he climbed the brae, unwind his bones and shed his span until, treetops his runway, he hit the skyline. For an instant he hung there—blonde hair silk on the wind. 'Syl,' I shouted, 'Syl, Syl, Syl,' and, my head spinning, I saw the sun—green-gold, blue cloud beyond—stand up on its hind legs to watch him on his way.

The Bracelet

'My God,' Aunty May said, 'when I think of that Roma Downes.'

She was home from The States again. Every second summer she came meaning to stay a couple of months but after a few weeks she'd suddenly pack and take a taxi to Dublin and fly straight back to Hartford. This country, she'd say, looking out at the rain pissing down, this country is for the mushrooms.

'When I *thinkovit*,' she repeated, nursing the cup of black coffee which was all she ever took in the mornings, sipping.

We were having breakfast together. The rest of the house had slept late.

'Yesterday?'

She'd been in Dublin yesterday.

'Yesterday,' she looked across at me, 'is right.'

I didn't say anything. She'd go on. Her small brown face shiny with cream, curlers beetling her hair that was auburn this time. Wisps of red touched the blue of her eyes.

'I went into Stinson's,' she put down the coffee-cup, tightened the belt of her white dressing-gown, lit a cigarette, 'to get the Beleek . . .'

The store smelled of—exquisite things. She loved handling the stuff, the glaze and the colours and the flower-decorations on the baskets. How in God's name they do it? The place was full of English. Madame? . . . Madame? . . . She picked the items carefully, listing her promises, then lost her head—the baskets—and went thirty dollars over her limit. So what, the place would get you—

'May!'

And there was Roma Downes. Swimming out of one of the big glass cases. Like a young rainbow trout. Or something.

'Roma, hi!' They shook hands. 'Well, how're *you* doing?' Wasn't she supposed to be in London? Model? Secretary?

'Great! You're home, May—for long?'

Roma thin-as-a-bootlace. Hair *bouffant*, face this month's Vogue—nearly. Still. That coat. And the shoes.

'Couple of months,' she scribbled the cheque, what age was Roma, nineteen, 'And how's Mother?'

'Mammy's marvellous.' Prancing on the long legs. 'Just back from The West. A fortnight over there.'

'You tell her I'll call by some of these days, won't you?' Not a bad looking girl. Except for the nose. 'Been rushing like mad since I got back, visiting, never had a second.'

'Sure. You're getting Beleek?'

'Can't resist it.'

''S beautiful. Love to have some. Sometime.'

They watched the man at the counter pack a magnificent creamer. The one for Lois. Roma murmured admiration but she could sense the lack of interest, their connection taking to the air, a thin smoke now, and beginning to nip—

'So—And what are you up to for the Summer?' They went to it again. 'Take a vacation yet?'

'No'—bubbling of a sudden—'Continent, with the boy-friend next month'—casual as you please, then qualifying—'Of course there's four in the party. Another pair.'

'Well, great,' she managed, 'Good for you. France, I suppose? Italy? You'll adore Florence. I was—'

'Sorry, May'—Roma was off—'There's Pauline.' A blonde

in slacks put her head in the door, chirped. 'Have to fly. See you. I'll tell Mammy. Bye!'

It was when Roma turned to wave from the door that she spotted the bracelet.

'Good-bye, Roma,' she worked up a smile that laddered instantly—'See you.'

The crowd reached for the two, grabbed, shunted them away.

'Your parcel, Madame.'

'My bracelet—'

'Madame?'

Well, of all the nerve—

'Would Madame care to—'

The Beleek.

'Oh—'

From behind his eyes the man watched her.

'May I have it shipped to Hartford?'

'Certainly, Madame.'

She gave him the address, paid the extra, and left.

'Wearing my damn bracelet,' Aunty May said, 'that I loaned her mother two years ago to wear at Tim Leonard's wedding.'

She took a long sip of the coffee. They were moving about upstairs. Flicking the windows, the day's first shower blew into the garden.

'Eighteen carat gold,' she said, 'I got it in Rome when I went for The Marian Year with Dot and Lois.'

She switched her eyes to the window, irritably searching. Green light spewed from the grass.

'It was a charm bracelet. You saw it? You remember it'—

I nodded. Vaguely, I did.

'And will you tell me,' she asked loudly, 'why people can't give these things back?'

'No manners'—I fumbled.

'Is right.'

'I was adding things to it,' she said, 'All the time. It had St. Peter's. And the Eiffel Tower.'

'Can't you—'

'I tell you I nearly got weak,' she said.

'Can't you get it back? Won't she'—

'Standing there chatting me,' she said, 'And my gold bracelet sitting on her arm.'

Her voice starting to ravel. Steps on the stairs, and my mother coming down the hall. She entered—'Good morning.' In the best of humour. Or prepared to be. I'd go.

'And what d'ye think,' Aunty May cried—for me, no pause, 'your Mother had to say when I told her of Roma, and the boy-friend and The Continent?'

By the door, my mother stood motionless.

'She said'—opposite me the small brown face smirked to mimic, ' "Oh, what matter. They've no sense at that age." '

'But that,' Aunty May rose and flung back her chair: she was a rod inside the white dressing-gown, and she picked up her cigarettes, stuck them in her pocket, never taking her eyes off me, 'that wasn't what they told us. Hurry home and bolt the doors was the line then. Mirrors to the wall, bend your knees and pray. Lies'—her voice splitting open—'And I wouldn't mind but they knew, they shaped the lie, and don't,' said Aunty May, her eyes wet and her mouth bright and her words a low terrible stitching, 'don't let them ever give that lie to you.'

She left and went straight up to her bedroom. Door-bang.

'Never mind her,' my Mother said, 'Poor thing's just upset.'

That afternoon there was sun for a change but sun chased by cloud. From early on, Aunty May was out in the garden.

Towards evening I happened to glimpse her from an upstairs window. She'd fallen asleep over a magazine. Wearing
a pink bathing-suit, she lay on her stomach, the white dressing-
gown thrown for a rug. Sun-glasses, netted pile of hair, white
shoulders and arms and thin white waist, and thighs and calves
white but veined, she lay, small, gathered, in the centre of the
garden. A loose fear beginning to slide and spread, I watched
until my taut breath blinded the glass.

Epithalamion

*S*aturday.

Dark reaches of nimbus cloud—edges fretted with warning—
were in sight early and shaping to great towered cumuli as
they piled up stores of thunder. About nine o'clock it began.
A livid stroke cut the clouds, branched, zig-zagged, died:
came the afterroll, crackling, clap and burst, peal and blast.
A pause. Then again the darting ribbons, incandescent, and
the following boom, rumble and roar to the scarred horizon.
Silence. Another slash—the triggered salute loud in the echoing sky.

On the wedding morning!

Did it spoil things, leave the guests uneasy? Not a bit.
Everyone knew they were made for each other, perfectly
matched.

'I never saw a couple so suited,' Rose O'Dowd kept saying
in the blustery porch of the church before the bride and groom
arrived, 'So completely suited . . .'

And all agreed. It was extraordinary.

'How did they meet?' somebody asked.

'How could they not have met?' was the protesting answer.

This was the mood, at the church, *en route* to the hotel,
while the storm flamed and rattled above. It was spilling rain.
Nobody cared. There's the car, run, no, it's not ours, quick,
now, here we go! The men, in sleek morning dress, petted
their lapels, shouted greetings over intervening heads, lofted

44

umbrellas gallantly: the women gabbled in strangely nunnish voices, clutched their hats and lost their handbags; running about on hunkers, the photographers smiled as if it were the sunniest day of the year . . .

Boom! the thunder called.

'Did you see the old woman?' Patsy O'Connell was asking in one of the taxis.

'*What* old woman?' demanded Miriam Brennan from the front seat where she sat pinned between the driver and Dorothy Slyne, who was not small . . .

'In the church,' said Patsy, breathless, always, eyes far open, thrilled that *she* had seen it, 'as they were coming down the aisle.'

Elf face poised, she stopped.

'Go on with it,' Miriam snapped, for everybody.

'The old woman stepped out—must have been—at *least* eighty, in rags, of course, there she was in front of them, I nearly fainted in the seat . . .'

'Well, what happened?' probed Dorothy.

'She took them each by the hand, wished them happiness, smiled this *incredible* smile'—Patsy's lashes leaped beyond surprise—'slipped into her seat again, and that was it—all in a second but it was the loveliest thing.'

She viewed her audience.

They were impressed.

'Isn't it just what you'd expect,' said Miriam, 'with this pair? They're special, born for each other.'

'Born for each other,' repeated Dorothy, in admiration.

The driver felt an obligation to confirm.

'They're a grand couple,' he said, latching the window against sheets of rain binding the city traffic-ways.

Into the plush dining-room of the hotel, the storm followed them. Through the consomme, the sole au vin, the Chicken

45

Maryland, and the Charlotte Russe, through the accompanying sherry, wines, and champagne, thunder stilled the clink of china and glassware, gashes of light skittered on the napery. It didn't matter. Everyone chatted away, cameras sizzled, the waiters were serene, long-armed, and, in the place of honour, no sign that the bridal pair were in the least upset.

'Celebration above,' O'Shea saluted, and Noreen—'I adore fireworks'—backed him up. Gay over the champagne, she toasted a wicked prong of lightning which, just then, snarled down to earth itself in the hotel garden.

In any event, when—at three o'clock—they set out on the honeymoon, the rain had stopped, and there was a glimpse of charred sunlight. Gathered on the steps to say good-bye, the crowd was boozy—the males all winking and slurred asides, the females mournful, *en garde*, as if readying themselves for some final deprivation.

'Brendan, come here a minute . . . Hold on there . . . Take your time now . . . No hurry . . !'

Several of his pals insisted on speaking to the groom, privately—and ostentatiously—before he left. Looking at Noreen, you could forgive this byplay: red hair which stopped short of flaming red, green, stormy, eyes, seagreen, a pleasant oval face, freckled but to advantage, and her body svelte, young—she was just twenty—made to be loved.

'Now, Noreen! Oooh! There it goes!'

To the spindrift cries of the girls, she threw her corsage, the spray of golden orchids soared, fell, bulbs flared again, there was a last douche of confetti, and the car was moving off, bound for the suburbs and the main road west. Into the traffic it twisted, halted at a crossing, went on, rounded a bend, was gone.

An instant before it rounded the bend, Sister Mary Clarinda —twenty-seven years in the Poor Clares—who was passing on the No. 10 bus, saw the car, saw the fall of confetti on roof and bonnet, looked for a moment into, sheer into, the eyes of the lovers. A moment. Past. She yearned, put by her yearning, stroked her rough beads, and promised them a bedtime prayer.

On the steps the guests remained, hesitant. Were they waiting for a photograph? With lace-trimmed hankies the women touched their eyes. The men looked as if they really must get busy about something—they didn't quite know what. And, the young crowd wondered, had anything been arranged? A dance, a get-together in somebody's flat, a show? Had anything been arranged? On the wet footpath confetti colours were beginning to run and mingle. Cars and buses went by in a foreign regular flow. A newsboy called the evening papers: his epicene wail melted the evening, blurred it to any October evening, lavender, vanishing and grey. Was it just now they'd seen the couple off?

'That lucky bastard, O'Shea!' said Frank Flanagan.

'Must have been a wedding!'

'Oh!'

The pair of typists delayed to watch. Furling the strip of carpet which extended from the hotel steps inward, the big commissionaire was bent, his face a mild rictus of exertion.

'Tonight's the night, tonight's the night,' sang Madeline, eyes on that wave of Cardinal Red, 'tum-tee-tum, tarrara tum-tee-tum.'

Joan gave her a coy grin, they both giggled, and danced home, especially happy they had Saturday dates.

'My God, weren't you glad to escape?'

'Glad!' he increased speed recklessly, 'I thought they'd eat us alive!' The car jounced, slithered over the sloppy midland roads, chugged through the occasional flooded stretch, broke free again, bucketed along with a zest that rang hilarity, the relief, of a couple honeymoon bound—a three day honey-moon, his teaching job would not permit more—and not to be subdued, not by floods, nor by mist churning the fields, nor by black returning rain.

There was incoherent talk of the morning.

'What kept you in God's name? You were'—

'They couldn't find the veil, the flowers were late, the taxi got caught'—

'Veil, flowers, taxi! Women!'

'And you! What about the ring? You took ten minutes'—

'The damn pocket was the size of a sack. How could'—

'Did you pay the verger?'

'The verger? Which was he?'

'In the sacristy, old, with the small face, and keyhole mouth'—

'I thought he was the Parish Priest.'

They laughed at the confusion, continued talking, sentences, question and answer, tumbling, until, at length, well on their way, tired with excitement, they fell silent.

'Any of them know what hotel?' she asked after a moment, softer.

O'Shea shook his head smugly.

'I ensured isolation, darling.'

A new mood opened and she moved over to feel that body hers. It had been a precipitous falling in love yet sullenly chaste. He'd fumed but Noreen—still trailing clouds of conventual glory—would not yield. Then the briefest engagement, hungering intolerably, and, tonight, coupling. Ears full of hymeneal explosions, aware distractedly of her soft rising breasts and young waist melting to girlish thighs, he sweetened with anticipation. All the pangs of denial rushed back but calm, he quelled them, rejoiced in the failing light of the late afternoon.

They were heading for Urchair Castle, about five or six

48

hours driving from the city, the route curling across the saucered centre of Ireland and up the slope to the mountains of the west. It was built on the edge of one of the great Connacht lakes, the lake, in popular tradition, a famous resort of the Vikings. O'Shea whose enthusiasms were quirky, was enchanted from the first.

'The Vikings, Noreen!'

She'd grimaced.

'Weren't they supposed to have butchered everyone?'

'Some Reverend Mother gave you that'—he was quick to reprimand—and told her of a history master he'd known who agreed with the textbooks . . . '*The Vikings, boys, raped Ireland*—' but insisted, lickerishly, that Ireland loved it, that wherever the Vikings arrived, the maidens—too long maidens —were waiting, beckoning, on the banks and on the shores . . . '*Don't boys, let us be too hard on the Vikings.*'

Now they were on the subject again. 'You'll see them tonight, Noreen, there on the lake.'

'Who?'

'The Vikings, of course, the fleet, prows high, faced for the shore.'

'And the maidens?'

'They'll be there too, I wouldn't be surprised, waiting, waving.'

'*The Vikings, boys raped Ireland,*' he intoned finally, in his voice a welcome for the Norsemen, allies now, it seemed in some eternal oceanic fray.

Intransigent, Noreen sniffed, and looked out the window. She still didn't think she liked the Vikings.

'We should be there by eleven,' he told her a short while later, 'If I can keep this speed.'

The needle was at sixty.

She made no reply, just watched him, hawkish features and blue turquoise eyes tensed towards the windscreen, shoulders, arms and wrists flexibly in command. Was she reading it correctly?—thrusting through the words, a male power that darkened to a threat as she pondered.

They hit a straight stretch: the needle rose to seventy. An hour further on, her unrest increasing, she saw the weepy lights of a town ahead.

'Athlone?'

'Yes, stop for dinner, darling?'

'Love to.'

Which cheered her, a change, something to diffuse the gathering fears—but immediately they were increased. Crossing the bridge (he was talking of wines, a glib irrelevancy no doubt meant to put her at ease) she had the misfortune to look down: the river was swollen, creamy under the lights, coursing turbulently. In that spumy flow there was a power, a raging, which, it seemed, must gulf her or else be unfulfilled.

Unreasonably afraid—they had parked the car by this time and were walking into the hotel—she had a picture, unrelated, of her mother, over the suitcase, arranging the satin nightgown bought for tonight, and there was pain, pain, in the gestures of folding.

'But of course, they won't have Traminer . . .' he was complaining authoritatively.

Before dinner they went to the bar for a drink. The barman's eyes awoke—

'Honeymooners?' he prepared the aperitifs, glancing at the scraps of confetti on the left sleeve of her suit.

The aroused eyes examined, smiled privately, established liaison with him, measured her.

'All before you now,' he announced, winked, and chuckled across the counter.

Furious she flashed a look at Brendan who took the protest blandly. Even defiantly. And she was shocked to discover how totally a *man* he suddenly appeared, male, dominant, undisguised.

The meal, inevitably, was ruined. Everyone knew, she reasoned, what tonight meant, and they let you know they knew, let you know with hints and sly looks and grins as they passed. The men, particularly, banded in some kind of spontaneous conspiracy which fired rebellion in lost corners of her being. Wildly she thought of Emily Pankhurst. Fright rose, focused in her eyes, the irises clouding to a deeper green, the circling rims of blue emerging sharply.

With magnificently ample gestures, O'Shea poured wine, ate the salmon, stored his strength for deeds ahead.

It was fifteen minutes to midnight when they reached the hotel. Passing through the unkept streets of a village clipped to the side of a hill, they saw an arched entrance. As they swung dangerously in, and up the avenue, low branches from bordering trees knocked on the roof, the clatter jarring.

Oh!

Stout and rambling it met them, ascending rows of mullioned windows, towers and turrets, the embrasures of the parapet limned against a clearing sky. Drawing across a cut-stone bridge and into the shadow of the battlements, they pulled up near the steps.

'It's not real!'

Looking out, he gave himself to the poetry of it: it was Diarmuid and Grainne, Tristan and Isolde, it was all the lovers of all the worlds. But—the realist in him—he had simultaneously a hot urge to carry her inside, above stairs, and let flesh have its way.

'Come on, Noreen.'

They got out.

While he hauled their cases urgently from the boot, Noreen looked up at the block of the building. Loosing a lemon dash of light on scrubbed stone, the door opened. A thin man in tousled livery hurried down.

'Mr. and Mrs. O'Shea'—they started at the unfamiliar address—he enquired, from behind long features and jutting eyes.

Yes.

The man, O'Shea noted, didn't look well at all. That cheese complexion: Danish Blue.

'Right.'

Agile enough, he collected the cases, and preceeded them up the steps. Noreen glanced at Brendan, and then at the porter. Under his jacket, the working of a pair of gaunt shoulders was visible. Above that, the back of his head, an oily grey, shelved acutely to a spindle neck.

He delayed to secure the door behind them.

'Just a minute.'

They were in the Reception Hall, puny before the scale and decor: above, an oak-panelled ceiling, opposite a superb Adams fireplace, to either side the walls panelled and hand-carved, doors here and there, a staircase rising from the right corner.

'We'll sign you up tomorrow,' the porter was saying matter-of-factly, 'I'll show you the room now.'

Inexplicably, the man reminded O'Shea—a tiny juggernaut tremor commenced inside him—of Pontius Pilate. There was no time to dwell on this. He led them across the parquet floor—their steps clacked against the quiet—and up the wide stairs, oak and deep-carpeted.

'It's No. 7,' the cinder voice announced when they reached the corridor. They looked uneasily at the sleeping doors.

Noreen nudged Brendan. He followed her eyes to the hands gripping the cases, bony, blue, and knuckly.

'No. 7. . .'

As he lowered the cases, the blades of shoulder shuttled. Showing them in, he positioned the luggage conveniently, and was at the door when O'Shea thought of the tip.

'Just a second.'

The nubbly hand closed on the coin.

'Thank you, Sir.'

Then—a neutral figure—the man was walking down the corridor and away.

Noreen was subdued—

'Quite a welcome.'

He nodded, closing the door.

Around them the castle was still.

Even before discovering the gilt-edged card on the dressing-table beside the bouquet of roses, they knew it was the bridal chamber. O'Shea was appalled. The room was large, carpeted in Persian blue, the velvet curtains also blue, the walls done in cream. A great bed—the fire blazing to the right of it—was lord of the place, the counterpane a cream brocade, the scented sheets turned back, and warm with reflections from the flames.

'Looks comfortable,' he said, when they caught each other staring. She went over and took up the card.

Tradition has long identified this room as the bridal chamber of Urchair Castle, and, in modern times, we have thought fit to nourish the custom. Think of it, therefore, or a place ancient—yet forever revivified. You, our guests tonight, will be part of it hereafter. We welcome you, and wish you success and happiness.

The Management

53

'Do it in style, don't they,' said Noreen, palely, as he read the script over her shoulder.

'Might as well, I suppose.'

He felt there was a cannon, close-range, levelled at his belly.

She vanished into the bathroom—O'Shea had turned away to hang up a suit—and locked the door. Undressing, he put on his pyjamas and dressing-gown, walked about, examined everything critically. He checked the wardrobes, opened several drawers, sat on the bed for a second and studied the fire, got up, looked out into the corridor and shut the door again, switched off all lights except two small reading lamps, came a second time on the message from the Management . . . 'a place ancient—yet forever revivified. . . .' Flittering the card, he let the shreds fall in the waste-basket. Again he looked up and down the space of the room. In those inset mirrors lay the records, and with the thought he had an impulse to move away from their curious gaze. His eyes fell on the roses, so *arranged*. It was all *arranged*, the scented sheets, the roses, the fire, everything. It was liturgical! Clinking on the shelf— probably—above the handbasin, he could hear the noise of God knows what item from her cosmetic bag.

'How are you in there?' he called.

'All right.'

She didn't sound it.

His dislike of the room growing, he could feel that juggernaut tic working up speed. Studious face wrinkled, he sat on the side of the bed nearest the fire. The springs purred. He examined the bed. Mattressed in depth, it had the scope of an arena. Its profusion chafed. Why hadn't they got a private room? Instead of one with a tradition which the management 'nourished'—and which you were part of 'hereafter . . .' Wisely the mirrors regarded him. Waiting for my next move, he thought. One of the windows rattled as the wind struck.

54

Noises busy in the bathroom, he went over and drew the curtains. There below was the lake.

Working the toothbrush slowly, she viewed her eyes in the mirror. They would never be the same again. It was his theory —and she inclined to accept it—that you could always tell from the eyes. 'Something goes from them, Noreen, *deflowered*, I suppose that's it.' She liked her eyes. In about a half-an-hour they would be changed unalterably. And next time she saw Mother, the evidence would be there, beyond hiding. God! Looking back at her, green and familiar and frightened, as if they knew their destiny. She swept the brush about her teeth, rinsed her mouth, turned away.

'There's a view of the lake, miles and miles of it.'

'Oh' . . . She stopped . . . 'Is it . . . is it beautiful?'

'Tremendous!' he said instantly, and she knew he hated it.

From the back of a chair, she took the white satin nightgown—hand-embroidered—and, recalled, again, her mother's pained hands over the suitcase. Putting it on, she felt the fine material cold against her skin. Aimlessly she tied the ribbon beneath her breasts. The cheval mirror drew her. Dismayed, she paused: the gown hung so loosely, did nothing for her, nothing, nothing, nothing. Burdened, she sat down, pulled on her blue kid slippers, disconsolately remembered the million conversations she and Patsy had spent on this subject.

'Where is your sense of the body, Noreen?'

'Body! Just look! Next thing I'll be on to padded bras!'

'Don't be an ass. Last month you thought you were huge. Next month'—

'All right, so I've got a figure like an accordion.'

'Stop it—that's not your problem at all. Look, do something for me—walk across the room, just walk across the bloody room, naturally . . .'

55

She would comply.

'Look! There it is!'

'What is?'

'It's the way you walk! Let yourself go, for God's sake!'

Those weekly arguments. All adding up to what? The fact that he would find her just plain uninteresting.

No sound in the bedroom.

She ran to the door, slipped the catch, opened it, and glanced out. He turned from the window.

'Despairing?'

Over his shoulder she saw Orion boldly straddling the sky.

'What in God's name are you at? You've been there the best part of an hour!'

'Won't be a minute.'

She shut the door again.

She put on the blue quilted robe with its shawl-collar of white lace. In the shop last week she'd loved it. Now it looked so damnably demure. Flecked with water, her watch lay on the ledge of the handbasin. She dried it, fumbled it on. Twelve-forty-five. In, say, twenty minutes time, all mystery destroyed. Pulling the robe tight about her, she tied it, and sat down for a second. She looked at the door. My God, suppose he went completely *male*—well, men did, didn't they? At times she had sensed an overpowering violence in him, something quite animal. Flinching, she got up, tidied the handbasin, rearranged the upset towels—and sat down again. Quite still, her eyes closed, she tried to remember all she had ever learned about it: remember, come on, remember, couldn't she remember something, a scrap even? Trapped, she found that it was wiped clear. All the information yielded by Sister Fidelma in those giggly biology classes at the Loreto, Stephen's Green, all the hints, postures, attitudes, uncovered in the occasional grubby novel, all the guidance from her mother's probing woman-to-woman talks—everything was gone. Stiffly she rose, and going towards the door, recalled—on the steps of the hotel—her virgin friends, hands vividly waving, and behind these hands, their bright bereaving eyes.

'Well, can you see your Vikings?'

He was at the window. She went over, and, his arm around her, they stood looking out.

'It's alive with them,' he announced dully.

The lake was partly visible. From below the window—lapping almost at the walls—it stretched until they lost its breathing surface, miles from where it met land. A distance out the moored islands lay like marauders. O'Shea's eye roamed in to the lake's edge, to the small area of garden between that and the building. He had the feeling of sudden activity down there. Moon and breeze coquetted with the young shrubs which tossed and soughed, fluttered and hushed, sank into tempting darkness. Had someone moved then—over to the right? Along the margin the riffled water jumped: he looked querulously out on the lake again: the islands, answering, by God, were making for the shore.

'I'll have my bath—just a shower.'

Kissing her, he turned his back on the lake, made for the bathroom. She heard the door close. What was that about? One of his moods, she decided. Before pulling the curtains she looked out but could see no Vikings. Only the aquagreen of the water, chill under the silver of moon.

When O'Shea emerged ten minutes later, she was in bed, lights off, and fire shadows jumpy on the high walls. Climbing in, he heard the pyjamas whisper against the sheets, felt the comfort of the silk against his skin. ('Your vestments, boy,' Donegan had insisted when he jibbed at the price—'Fit robes for such an hour.') Known perfume greeted him, and with a bravado flip he pulled up the bedclothes.

At his touch she turned. They moved together, embracing.

'Relax, darling.'

'I *am* relaxed.'

They separated.

'You're frozen,' he sympathized, accusingly.

'I'm frozen!'

Limb to limb they moved together again, coaxing their bodies towards passion. Panicked, O'Shea felt for his member. Dead. Jesus! A warrior without a spear. Still patient, he caressed, they fondled, stroked flesh. Nothing happened. Not a stir. Frightened they paused.

He doesn't desire me, she grieved.

Stunned, he lay beside her.

Neither said a word.

In the fire a coal shifted. The flames sprang.

They resumed after a few seconds, groping, searching, *willing* their bodies to respond. Frantic they entwined.

Scared they lay back.

'Why don't you want me?'

'You know I want you,' he snapped, 'I don't know what's happened, we're both *ice*.'

Shadows polished the silence.

'Noreen?'

They began afresh. Brutally he tried to pressure energy towards his smitten loins. Her body meaningless, she waited. Nothing doing. For a half-hour they fumbled as if puberty had fickly renounced them, withdrawn all its favours. Astonishment was twisting to fear when they heard a sound. It seemed to come from beneath a window left slightly open —a broken gasp followed by a spill of girl's laughter.

'One of your Vikings, I suppose,' she suggested—and they

fled into laughter, high, prolonged, in which they met again the events of the day, heard the room fill with cries of couplings past, caught even the noise of keels harsh on the eager stones. O'Shea had the charity to forgive—almost—his quisling phallus. Deep in laughter, and exhausted, she heard him say... 'Tomorrow, Noreen?' and 'Tomorrow,' she agreed.

His last memory as chuckles died to sleep was of a mirror's waiting face, shadows spraddling the opposite wall, and, on the dressing-table, the white of roses.

Once during the night she awoke, cried a while, then fell back to sleep.

Sunday

O'Shea awoke at ten-thirty, saw the sun chinking past the curtains, and was immediately resentful.

It was a wonderful morning.

Beside him she lay quietly but her sleeping face was a set frown. Looking about the room he discovered it even more depressingly bridal than before. He thought of last night. Exhaustion. And the way it had finished. A good job they'd been able to laugh: he could recall with no trouble a slack empty fear.

Stumbling out of bed, he went to the window and drew the curtains. The lake was calm, blindingly happy in the sun. Far out, he saw the island fleet, clustered and at rest—

'Oh, it's a lovely morning,' he heard, behind him.

Amused to find in it his own depression, he turned, went over, kissed her, saw last night's bewilderment in her eyes. They laughed wryly.

'We were just too tired,' she said eventually.

'Exhausted.'

'You sleep well?'

'Fine.'

59

(O'Shea had slept badly, experiencing an endless and parching dream which abandoned him in some stony desert.)

'You, darling?' he asked.

'Not bad . . . feel much better now.'

Why not now, then?

Without hesitation, he decided. No, not now, tonight's the time, tonight. The decision was bitchy. Looking for thorns, he hadn't missed the one jab of accusation her eyes—a moment back—had not been able to subdue.

'You never saw anything like the lake,' he side-tracked.

'Let's have a look.'

Her face darkened before the blazing water. Relenting, he took her in his arms.

'Tonight, Noreen.' She nodded, hugged him shelteringly, then cart-wheeled to gaiety—

'Brendan, breakfast in bed! We can get Mass at noon. Ring the bell—there's lots of time.'

She was right.

Commandingly, O'Shea rang the bell.

In response, a uniformed (navy-blue and gold braid) boy appeared. He must be thirteen or fourteen, though small and slight, a buttony figure, the double row on his chest extending to the features, button-mouth, button-nose, button-eyes. And blond cherub hair.

'Morning.'

Soprano, shy and forward: pert glances took them in, balanced them, curiously.

'Like breakfast up, sir?'

Something about the imp tickled Noreen. Under the blankets she elbowed Brendan. No answer. He was watching, sober-faced.

Something about the imp. As he took the order, his eyes sprang back to her, rested on her bare arms—'Orange juice for two'—on her covered bosom—'And cornflakes?'—on her face, her hair—'Coffee, eggs and bacon'—the eyes now shining hazel . . . 'Morning paper?' It was exactly like watching someone fall, headlong slowmotion, in love. On that angel face it was irresistible!

'Julia will have it right up, Sir.'

Smiling, glances fading farewell, he left.

'The little brat!'

'Oh, he's not a bad child,' she provoked, 'Polite, knows his place, what do you want?'

'Didn't you see him? He almost stripped you!'

'Nonsense . . . he's hardly out of the cradle.'

'Out of the cradle! That child's dreams are insatiable!'

She let him simmer to silence. Fair enough. If he wanted it that way. But the incident had pleased her tremendously. Well, it *was* funny, the hazel eyes, and the fall, headlong, slowmotion.

He boiled over again—

'You needn't romanticize it. He's at the moment of terror, sheer terror, finding himself corners where he can wonder just what it's all about.'

She yawned, stirred in the bed, and took up a comb. Its supple swing and pull, the knowing that—coiffured on Friday —her hair was at its best, gave her an honestly sensuous thrill. Like the feel of nylon—sliding the stockings on and up— against calf and thigh. She noticed the sun, canary, warm, and singing, on the blue of the carpet. How strong was that sun? Would it give a tan? She examined her arms, where the August brown—doggedly gained on the beach at Tramore —now barely showed.

'Would that sun tan, Brendan?'

He looked at her, at the window—and Julia, the promised Julia, arrived with breakfast.

Behind a large tray—which wasn't for a second allowed to dominate—she entered.

'Morning,' said Julia, closed the door with a judged tap of the heel, and came forward like a collaborator.

They smiled limited greeting.

Julia was twenty-five or six, big, brown-haired, had a fresh complexion, hot eyes, a squab nose, and wide welcoming mouth.

'I hope you were comfortable,' she lilted, arranging things. They were comfortable.

'Lots of the honeymooners has this room,' said Julia, standing back, shrining the bed with her hot eyes.

'Yes, it's the bridal chamber,' O'Shea growled. They tasted the fruit juice.

'You came from Dublin?' she crossed the room with a buttocky walk to draw the curtains properly, 'About twelve o'clock?'

'Yes.'

Against the window Julia angled her bosom: breasts which foamed. 'I saw the car,' slyly, 'and the lights coming on . . . Saturday nights is active in these parts,' she added in explanation, whirled the curtains.

Noreen drained her glass.

'A lovely view of the lake,' said Julia, rampant in the sun. Yes, it was.

'Well,' she swivelled from the window, came over, 'two is company.' She blessed them with her smile. 'You'll ring if you want me?'

Certainly.

'Sure you have everything now?'

'Everything's fine,' O'Shea insisted.

'Just ring the bell.'

A final view of Julia's big body and roundly strapping thighs. She was gone.

For a minute they said nothing.

'You see her eyes, Brendan?'

Noreen streamed milk over the flakes.

'I did.'

'Well?'

'A long time ago, a long time ago.'

They continued breakfast, morose.

The priest, on his way to the altar, halted to address three grandfathers lurking on the threshold.

'*Come up!*'

Advancing a few yards, the three found hiding in the lee of a pillar beside the confessional.

Ascending the steps, the priest came back down, and began Mass: an old man, crimson bald, his light figure stooped, a drowsy aura containing him as he sighed the Latin and raised the Missal pages with curled baby hands.

Making themselves comfortable in the cribbed seats, O'Shea and his bride prayed in desultory fashion, slid into the sluggard ease of the gathering, composed—queerly—of the very young and the very old. From the eastern windows, four broad sunbeams lowered their lulling wands, motes in a dreamy flow, until it seemed that but for one weak-eyed man, recalcitrant, who insisted on making the Stations of the Cross while Mass went on—but for his distracting progress, celebrant and congregation might have lazed into a tapestry of sleep and held these attitudes forever.

Mass was two-thirds over when she heard him whisper —'Watch this.'

It was time for the sermon.

The priest removed his chasuble, came down the altar and genuflected, the alb bandaged about his thin frame. Tetchy steps sounded on the tiles. He climbed into the pulpit.

Noreen smiled, was aware again of the drift of odours—
clay and lodged sweat and brilliantine—put aside her prayer-
book and sat back for the performance.

The congregation still dozed. Rather the elders did. The
children looked about for something to do. Anything. In a
seat beside the pulpit a small boy commenced dismantling
his mother's beads, breaking the links with care, then thriftily
dropping each bead into his trousers' pocket. Through one of
the sidedoors, half open, came the colourless chirping of a
sparrow.

'There is a Beast always within us,' the preacher cried, 'and
let that Beast be tamed!'

Along the benches there was a stirring. Someone persuaded
the recalcitrant to sit down.

'You know of your pleasuring, your lusts, your brute joys.
They come easy to you—these things of the devil— and you
steep yourselves in them!'

Men and women, the bent and the grey, roused themselves.
A red excitement rose in the pale face of the accuser. He knew
what was going on, what *must* go on, among the shameless who
took such joy in their frisking bodies. And if they wanted him
to say where, he *would* say, he would point to the stained
couches of copulation in his parish—the hedges! the very
hedges, the haysheds, and the barns!

From triangular sockets his eyes flamed like an Inquisitor's,
the shoulders reared, the baby hands fluttered beyond control.

The audience gave full attention. In the front seat an old
couple preened, shifted in unconscious applause. While,
collecting remembrance cards, children feasted over the misty
faces of the dead.

—'Will you never kennel the animal within you?'

From the empty gallery at the back, the question rever-
berated, the reaching ears of the old caught it, preacher and

audience closed in a tussle, intimate and prolonged: the voice, spiralling, drew—who can tell what the listener hears? —night noises out of the air: crossroads cries before the scattering for home, the swing of unoiled gates on quiet lanes, the fall of steps on twisty farmhouse stairs.

—'If you must then, let the Beast devour you, body and soul . . .'

An hour passed before this passion failed, and priest and people, flushed, released their mutual hold.

Five minutes later, Mass was over.

The honeymooners went out into the white day, hurried from the pensioners grouping beneath the yews, and made for the Castle gates.

'What time is it, Brendan?'

He checked—

'One-thirty.'

They walked on more slowly.

'I thought,' she hesitated, 'he'd never stop.'

O'Shea said nothing.

She looked at him.

He had nothing to say.

'That bloody bitch!'

It was evening—the Television Lounge had sheltered them painfully for the afternoon (what, in any case, do you *do* on a honeymoon when you're not doing what you're supposed to do?) and they had come upstairs to dress for dinner.

In the room, Julia's tracks were everywhere—the fat furl of the sheets, the noisy fire, the privacy of drawn curtains, the almost replenished fragrance of the roses. It made Noreen edgy too.

'Brendan, should I? The green? The beige? No, I hate it. What about the brocade? Do I need a stole?'

'For God's sake, wear that, it's perfect,' he interrupted, when—pulling on the gold brocade sheathe, she changed dresses for the third time.

'It's not perfect'—she spun around—'it's a dress I dislike intensely, I don't know why I bought it.'

In the same breath she decided to wear it, sat down at the dressing-table, her back to him, and thumped the powderpuff against her cheeks. Why did it have to be like this—so jittery? This was marriage? Maybe the meal would help. And they could both do with a couple of drinks. Putting aside the powderpuff, she stared her unaltered eyes and fumbled for the lipstick.

On the corridor they met the porter, padding along like someone who had not been permitted a destination. He gave them his hyperthyroid glance, passed on.

He was linking her, irritably.

'Now, what's wrong?'

'It's the damn stairs—they take you over!'

'Stop being helpless, Brendan.'

But he was right about the stairs: they swooped to the hall, routed you to the dining-room beyond, flung open the doors, dramatized your arrival. And evening wear put you at the mercy of such an enemy, gave you a clinging sense of shame.

Crossing the hall, entering, they were placed at a table near the door. No one noticed their coming in. They examined the menu, ordered steak, and had a Martini each while adjusting to the atmosphere.

'Lovely.' Noreen twirled the olive—'Just what I need.'

O'Shea tasted his.

'Aren't the candles beautiful?'—her eyes were rambling the room.

'Sure,' he granted.

She looked about again, nervously intrigued.

66

At almost every flickering table there was a couple, mostly older couples—men and women in their thirties and forties, a fine experience somehow conveyed by the poise of those groomed heads, even more by the odd fling of laughter. It would have been a relaxed scene but for one thing, the purling, pulsing ovals of flame, golden yellow, straining. Between each leaning pair this urgent breath stirred, until, it seemed that the low voices belonged to shadows, and that both, shadows and voices belonged to mesmeric purl and pulse which topped the sticks of tallow.

'Which wine, Noreen?'

He was eyeing the list, choosily.

'Some Burgundy, Brendan, you pick one.'

His fingers hunted among the Burgundies.

She was watching a couple two tables away. The man looked English, in his thirties, heavy, redfaced, moustached. The woman, about the same age, was pale, blonde, beautiful. She wore a silk print dress, and a mink stole lay delicately against her slender arms.

'Mr. and Mrs. O'Shea?'

It was the Manager, so flexibly polite, so astutely bowing. 'They were comfortable?'

Of course.

Certain?

Everything was fine.

Was there anything *he* could do to make their stay more enjoyable?

In the shadows, O'Shea winced.

No, not a thing, thank you.

The hotel particularly liked to have honeymooners among the guests.

Oh?

Yes, it added a certain, how would you put it, well how

67

would you put it, it brought people back to their own honey-moons, the early joy and all that. There was no doubt about it, either, it did add something, he'd seen it—had they ordered, by the way, been cared for?

Yes, they had.

(Bright face glistening, haste in his gestures, the English-man was gulping oysters.)

Good. Fine. Good-bye for now. He would see them again.

'You really hungry, Noreen?'

If they would pardon him?

The Manager was back. With a well-pressed smile.

One question?

Of course . . .

He had almost forgotten: how had they liked the bridal chamber?

Wonderful, O'Shea assured him.

And the bride?

The bride loved it.

That was all he wished to know. Au revoir.

A ringmaster pleased, he sidled away.

'Am I really hungry? I don't know . . . I'd love another drink.'

They had another Martini each.

Reaching across the table, the Englishman took the woman's hand, stroked as if it were her whole body. She allowed him this. Watching—at the same time keeping up an uncertain conversation with Brendan—Noreen saw the woman then free her hand, take a cigarette from a gold case. Abruptly, the man, eyes hurried, lips and teeth dark with wine, pulled a candle from its holder and offered it. The small flame purred: a smear of wax lipped over, streaking the smooth side down almost to the thick red fingers.

'With the compliments of The Manager.'

A waiter placed two more Martinis before them.

O'Shea had lost his appetite early. A trolley of hors-d'oeuvres set him off: slick green olives with red pimento tongues, celery sticks loaded with creamed cheese, plump kosher pickles, *pâté de foie gras*, rich quivery aspics, cucumbers in sour cream, and pellets of caviar. Above the tray a sickly relish of odours. And then, the fat-heaped food on every table —roast beef (juices running, grease glinting on the juices), liver and kidney, sweet-breads, loin-chops, broiled lamb, veal, the reek of garlic, mint and gravy, something animal in the gusto of the feasting.

'My God, it's gross!'

'What's gross, Brendan?'

'This banqueting'—her attention swung back to the Englishman, the woman—'it's disgusting!'

But the medicinal fumes of the gin and vermouth helped, and he was finished his third drink when—as if he had just sat down—it came to him; she looked superb in that brocade, the sheathed lines, soft rising breasts and young waist melting, melting, melting. His body flared. Now, now, you damn fool, now's the time, leave, take her upstairs . . . 'Noreen,' he reached for her arm, 'let's go now.'

'But the meal?'

'To hell with it!'

'It won't look'—

'Who gives a curse?'

'But they'll all *know*?'

'Well, who cares? C'mon.'

She vacillated.

'Steak for two.'

Baulked, they watched the waiter serve the steak, arrange layers of garnishing. O'Shea sampled the Mâcon and approved.

The waiter left.

'To later.'

Overloudly they clinked the toast.

He studied her. Was she looking a little . . . Well . . . Her face somehow *slanted*? Was it slanted? Or was that his eyes? The place had grown quiet. Did drink make you deaf? He could see camp fires all over the dining-room. Wigwams. 'Horrible steak,' he prodded, 'how's yours?'

'Not hungry,' she poked a mushroom free, nibbled it, 'just a little more wine, please, I like wine.'

'But I poured'—

—'Gone . . . just a little, teenyweeny.'

She let him brim the glass.

Listening to the thirsty gurgle, he gave himself more. 'Your cheeks are flushed,' he cautioned, levelling his eyes to examine her, 'is that desire?'

She giggled.

'Let's go now, c'mon, Noreen.'

'The bill, Brendan, you must sign for the bill. Like a gentleman.'

Mystified, he pondered a red spreading stain on the cloth. A map of where? His glass had heeled over. He placed it upright. Poltergeists were roguish little ghosts. Roguish little ghosts.

'What bill are you referring to?'

Refilling the glass, he stared pompously across.

'For the meal'—she waved her drink in explanation—'Gentlemen never'—

—'Oh, the meal!'

He had forgotten the meal.

'Well, for God Almighty's sake!'

That clubroom voice wasn't his, wasn't hers. He looked up. Tim Mulcahy, a college friend of the past, watched the sporty eyes gambol over Noreen.

'You lucky bastard, O'Shea!'

'Sit down for a drink.'

Mulcahy had already drawn up a chair. Don Juan Mulcahy of the Medical School. Whom he had never liked.

'Well, of all things. Meeting you two here.' He smiled. 'Enjoying yourselves?'

They nodded: reticent.

'Where did you go today?'

The Television Lounge.

The Television Lounge?

Mulcahy finished the Mâcon puzzling over this.

O'Shea ordered liqueurs.

'I went beagle hunting with Dolores, what an evening! We started off . . .'

The rough country, the smooth, the crowd, the pace, the girls, how finally the hunt had ended for Dolores and him in a well grassed hollow which obligingly trapped the sun . . . 'We simply couldn't go any further, just lay there,' he admitted triumphantly. 'Really marvellous evening.'

He left them to join Dolores—she was 'resting,' and, as he did, Noreen saw the Englishman, arm about the woman stepping upstairs.

'The lounge,' O'Shea directed, 'just a drink to finish off.' He had to get the taste of Mulcahy out of his mouth.

Coming bumpily to land on a couch in the lounge, they had a couple of whiskies each, talked in bleary tones of the elegant life, argued over a gargoyle head—it scowled from an opposite corner—which Noreen insisted was Elizabeth I but O'Shea claimed was the last High-King of Ireland, tried to focus the other guests moving sure-footed about, ordered a brandy to steady up, and at about ten o'clock—setting the snifters aside—faced for the stairs.

Quite drunk, with puffy challenging faces, they walked out, crossed the hall, and stopped.

71

'Such stairs.'

'How?' he asked, and gripped the newel as if to test its reality. 'So big!'

The evening had put a soggy weight on her heels. Rashly she looked down at the Italian shoes, something up-ended behind her eyes, she grabbed his arm for support—

'S big all right.'

'An' I feel boobulous,' she complained.

'Boobulous?'

'Very boobulous.'

'Me too,' O'Shea said agreeably, 'I feel decidedly boobulous.' He noticed it then: the stairs were in motion. The stairs were going upstairs. And the squiggy pattern on the carpet was in motion too. Which proved it. He could see it quite clearly. You had only to step on.

'Now, look.' He told her what to do as they stood there holding warmly to the sustaining newel. 'You just step on an' it brings you up.'

Clambering, they ascended slipslap, fell several times—the carpet glided icily from their feet, recovered, at length made the plateau of the landing. Looking down like Alpinists they saw the porter standing beside the fireplace, viewing them superiorly.

'Bastard,' said O'Shea.

''S right,' she confirmed.

On a muzzy course they progressed along the corridor.

'Boobulous!' Noreen giggled as they reached the door of No. 7, 'boobulous, boobulous, boobulous!'

'Me too,' he supported her weakly, 'I feel distinctly boobulous.'

Within, with dissolving fingers, they undressed, and collapsed to a drunken sleep.

On the lake Vikings were romping madly for the shore.

Monday

During the night, tumultuously sick, they both endured long spells of retching. Late next morning, they awoke to meet the hangover.

'How are you?' O'Shea enquired—rhetorically.

She shivered down in the bed. Under each closed eye lay a blotch of fatigue, hyacinth, unambiguous. And in the back of his skull a pigmy gang was mining, their incessant picks needling flinty pains.

'What kind's the day?' she asked.

Morbidly he estimated the light.

'Looks cold.'

Hugging the blankets, she hid in a half-doze. With instant cruelty his thoughts arranged themselves.

The last day.

And you haven't done it yet.

You poor ineffectual bollocks.

He stared about the room. On the dressing-table sat the roses. The mirrors ringed him like witnesses. Beside him she lay queasy, exhausted.

'Noreen?'

'Yes.'

A flatness in the voice. She opened her eyes.

'Now?'

'But we're both feeling wretched—No, Brendan, let's tonight. Not now. Please.'

Yet he knew he must try, he had to. Roughly he took her to him so that she was startled but, quickly submissive, gave herself. He clung, turned soul, mind, body to coupling, held her desperately, thought of hot mounting flesh, thought, visioned, remembered, until it seemed the very power of imagination must raise him to success. Was something happening? His heart catapulted. At last? Sceptical, he

73

paused, checked. A slack sail in a boundless calm. O'Shea you're finished. But the evidence worked contrarily, would not let him desist. Resuming, he played her with twisting fingers, lay close, let his limbs roam hopefully, gave every sinew to the struggle, and once, miraculous, almost raised sail but, in the end, gave up.

'Don't worry, Brendan'—the same voice—'It'll be all right tonight.'

Nailed to his cross, eyes on the ceiling, he kept seeing the gargoyle faces which peopled the lounge. Those spouty faces, Austrian oak, looking down as if they knew.

'Let's go down to breakfast. Okay?'

A new reasonable voice.

Indulging his crucified pose, he listened suspiciously.

'Please, Brendan, we might as well enjoy the day.'

With an ease the perversion of relaxation, she got out of bed, put on her dressing-gown, and went into the bathroom.

He kept his eyes on the gargoyle faces, multiplying as he watched. 'And better move fast,' she called from inside, 'before Julia arrives.'

He listened to the spewing taps, a flutter of steps on the corridor, a brush racketing against the skirting-board a few doors down. Now you know, he told himself, now you know: he had often speculated on how it must have been for the castrati, choiring out their shrill lives in the dim lofts of St. Peter's. The poor unfortunate bastards! Levering himself up, he threw aside the clothes, swung his legs off the bed, and sat there a few minutes, shoulders turning cold, in his crotch a dry emasculated pain. On the way below they saw Julia, bouncy on a far-off landing. She was talking to one of the younger maids, a slight uplooking girl, and over the two— they were loading a cupboard from the fat linen basket between them—floated Julia's petticoat laughter.

The dining-room was fatigued, full of Monday morning. Most of the guests had already breakfasted, so that among the few regulars, they noticed the newcomers at once.

'Company for us,' Noreen remarked.

Another honeymoon couple. You just knew. They had probably arrived last night. The bride was in her thirties, plain, provincial, the grey woollen dress—especially with those country hips and pudding shoulders—badly chosen, her posture, her movements, stiff with gaucherie. Paunched in a dark featureless suit, the groom was forty or thereabouts, his full face behaving itself now, used to behaving.

'Quite a pair, by God,' was O'Shea's sour verdict, 'twenty years of cautious courting, I'll bet.'—Noreen was unresponsive —'No bloody wonder they look like pilgrims.'

Still no response from Noreen. She was studying the couple. 'Well?'

'Well, what?' she turned to him.

'What are you thinking?'

'You can't guess?'

He followed her eyes across and then, with a curdling start, saw what she meant, what he had missed. It was in the way they ate for one thing, easy and eager, satisfaction and appetite, mingled, contentedly there. And it was about them in other ways also, for all their tame appearance, if you watched the man, particularly, something, the bulge of his forearms, the slant of his head, some supple quality contradicting the mass of him. O'Shea was flooded with resentment. The conqueror. With a belly on him like a harvest frog and that confraternity face. Noreen nibbled toast with a fine air of vindication.

'Eat up, Brendan,' she advised.

Occupied, he let it pass, watched the pair. They were already finishing breakfast, prudently folding the napkins octavo, putting them aside, rising, settling their chairs, and

going towards the door. O'Shea's face shifted at the sight—
that crippled gait as the man dragged his right leg in the
slow clubfoot limp of deformity.

'Jesus,' he muttered, 'Oh, sweet Jesus!' transfixed by the
halting rhythm of their going.

After breakfast, indecisive, they retreated to the bedroom.
Coming upstairs, Noreen had felt healthier but when he sat
down, alien, lit a cigarette and began to read the morning
paper, her confidence cracked. She snatched a pair of nylons
—'Better wash these'—went into the bathroom, and shut the
door. Fixing the stopper of the handbasin, she tossed the
stockings in and ran the taps. Hands active, she took the soap,
swished up some suds, flopped the stockings about, turned off
the taps when the overflow began to whine. Prisoned, she
looked up at the window. God, if she'd only known what it
would be like! Imagine ten, twenty, thirty years of this.
Abruptly tired, weak indeed, she moved to the chair and sat
down, fingered her thighs, tender to touch. She rose, caught
her eyes in the mirror, fled at once from the reflection. She
emptied the basin, rinsed the stockings, rolled them in a towel,
flung them over the shower-rail, and letting the taps run—
she needed that noise—sat on the edge of the bath, thoughts
racing for exits.

What are you going to do?

Well . . .

Do you know?

Couldn't we . . . we live together as companions, forget the
whole business and behave like human beings?

Are you joking?

Lots of people probably do—even if they don't broadcast
it.

You think he'd agree?

76

I . . . I don't know.

Oh, you know all right.

I can try it.

Don't waste your time.

She could hear him moving about in the room, steps determined and restless.

So? What else?

I could call it off.

What?

The marriage.

How call it off?

It's not—consummated. They have a law, there's a church law.

Talk sense for a change.

What do you mean?

You love him, don't you?

I . . . suppose so.

And he loves you?

Ask him. I don't know. He's in there.

Loving?

Worried.

About whom?

About himself, his missing manhood.

Not about you?

No, about nothing else, nobody else.

Selfish?

And callous.

Like a man?

She heard the rustle of a newspaper as he took it up, sat down again to read. Something accusingly overbearing in even that sound. Why was it that the more he failed, the more untouchably superior he became?

And tonight? Can you face him?

Can't say . . . I—
Can you face him?
You can't answer a question like that until the time—
Can you face him?
No.
I thought as much. You can't.
No.

With merciless jealousy, she grudged a million women their lovers, and she grudged a million million women their secure virginity, she grudged and her heart strained at the injustice. What about *her*. The water continued flowing in bright gushes and the white bathroom tiles magnified to huge sterile slabs of cold.

You're in a fix, you know?
All right, I'm in a fix.

A cold bathroom, a cold day, and your husband in the next room. Cold. He *is* your husband?
Yes.
Whom you love?
You asked me that.
Whom you love?
I've told you, isn't once enough?
You do love him then?
Yes.
And he loves you?
He did . . .
But does he?
I don't know.
You're right, you don't, why not admit it?
Admit what?
Go on, admit it.
I said I don't know, I don't know, *I don't know*.

The white surrounding slabs were whirling with the

78

questions in her mind, and the pale answers were lost in the whirl, she felt a hysterical chill all over, while, inside her or beside her, the cutting dialogue of the last five minutes was being played back, and, then, at its height, interrupted by a *crack*, sharp, whippy, as he shifted the newspaper pages. She heard it again: crack. The sound was male, riven with intolerance and assertion, and it decided her.

She went back in.

'Lost my lipstick,' (the lie rose adroitly from her panic) she told him—going from the room—'must have dropped it below somewhere.'

'Okay.'

From behind the newspaper.

'Back in a second.'

She closed the door, perspiration on her palm, and made for the stairs. Where will you go? Have you any idea? None, just to go somewhere, get out of here, anywhere, away from him because she was wretched and it was a failure and he loved no one, no one but himself. Downstairs, she hurried across the hall, thank God for the careless trick he had of leaving the key in the switch, pushed open the big door, and went out. She spotted the car, parked some yards away, on its own, waitingly, and, hastening across the gravel, she found herself seeing it, yes, waitingly, as she had seen it a thousand times from the window of her flat, watched it, watched him, there in the seat, smoking casually as the traffic passed, waiting for her, looking up when she opened the door and came down the steps, their eyes beginning to talk over the heads and through the people passing on the footpath, and—she was beside the car.

The empty seat, the steering wheel, the dashboard, the key, looked out at her. She turned and went back towards the entrance, the crunch of her footsteps newly loud as the galloping within her began to still.

79

'Let's get to hell out of here for a few hours. How about a drive?'

He spoke from the window as she came in.

'Sure'—there was a fuzz of treachery on her tongue—'I'm all for it.'

'The way you said that!' he rounded on her.

She quailed, came over contritely. 'I'm sorry, Brendan, I do want to go.' She was beside him, and he held her a moment in an unsettled embrace.

'Okay . . . let's go. C'mon.'

They separated, grabbed coats, went below and out to the car with hunted steps. Driving down the avenue, O'Shea turned left at the gates, committed them to going westward. Not far off, he could see the lake, the islands, the rumpled shore. He looked away. They passed through the village, and he made a right turn.

'To the mountains?'

He nodded, already relaxing, gazed over the dark countryside and toward the low merging slopes.

'We need this. Let's forget the Castle, give ourselves to the spaces, air, the light, everything.'

As he said it, he had a cynic recognition of the absurdly pantheistic tone. You're far gone, O'Shea, he thought, but she seemed responsive and, in a twist of self-mockery, he developed the theme, using a very poor lecture he had once heard an art critic deliver on 'The Last Light of Europe: A Connacht Prism,' and misquoting several lesser known Synge poems. No harm done. The effect was vaguely curative and some kind of escape seemed possible when, an hour after midday, the sun seeped between clouds, shadows began to run on the mountains, the rolling line now cinnamon, purple, russet, now luminously mauve, as if some Godalmighty Picasso perched above, drunkenly dealing beauty.

It couldn't last.

They started to meet the children, infant figures, early free from school, rumble-tumble, raggle-taggle, the facile spawn of men. At once O'Shea was on the defensive. Every heedless face was strident with accusation. His pain livened, the colours fell, hid in the hills.

'Brendan, *please*. Don't brood like that.'

His head full of the child gabble, he couldn't hear her. More of them now, harumscarum, wild over the road. Could men breed so casually? Seed be so fluid? Watching the children, his mind following them into the flanking valleys and the busy places of their making, he grouched to silence at the day's deception. She tried to rouse him. No good. He drove, transferring his frustration to the almost undirected, spinning, wheels. The afternoon spun grey shadows without let-up. A couple of hours later they topped a hill. Ahead lay a barrier. O'Shea—darkly pacified by the sight—eased down the slope, a quarter-mile. They came to the beach, the swelling tide— green waves lunging, and, beyond, the giant miles of the Atlantic.

The tyres scrunched on a ridge of gravel and shells which backed the cusp of sand, and he stopped the car.

'Might as well get out, I suppose,' he reached for the door-handle.

So they got out, stood there moodily, the sea-air saucy, sea-sounds collecting, the slap and rasp of the waves, the shrapnel cries of the black-backed gulls. Then they walked to a litter of rocks and sat together on one, slumped, stared at the nothing of the horizon.

'Couldn't we talk about it?'—he spoke eventually.

'What's the use?'

'It might help me, that's all.'

'Go on.'

Eyes intent on the pointless pattern, she was brushing her foot against the sand.

'Well, for Christ's sake, what's gone wrong? It was never like this before.'

'I know.'

'Why now? I still want you.'

'You're sure?'

'Of course, I'm sure.'

Her eyes remained on the shoe whorling the sand. Scrabbling, a dozen gulls winged heavily down, primped on the waves.

'Look, I've tried to help, I've tried,' her thrashing foot splintered a nest of shells—'but'—

'But what?'

'We wanted too much . . . we . . . we can't be natural.'

'All right! Let's be natural!' he gibed. 'Let's strip and make love here—roll in the bloody sand!'

She followed, distantly, the shifting patina on the water.

'Don't you see?' he lashed, 'I feel like a damn eunuch, and I know I'm not!'

'What am I supposed to do? Play whore?'

'That's right! Make it dirty. The Irish virgin at bay, by God!'

'Stop it.'

She stood up and clutched a face of boulder, looked so suddenly frail and cornered that regret seared him.

'I'm sorry.'

She didn't turn.

A light wind blew, sustaining the gulls, the tide came on, the mile of beach to each side was empty, empty to the limits of scrub and cliff except for the car twenty yards back.

'Noreen?'

Still she didn't turn.

He looked morosely along the strand, and then, her hand on his wrist, she was beside him—'We have tonight yet.' With him again now, softly, her fingers inside his open collar, against the lie of his neck, coaxing. Loosening her jacket, he drew her to him, felt the flow of her waist, the lithe movement of her shoulder as she planed, delicate and easing.

Now?

Her eyes rose to him and she nodded, looking about, asking silently, where? He glanced towards the car, and they ran, sand slopping into their shoes. Fumbling to undress they got into the back seat. Peeping-tom gulls hovered. Breathless at the glory of his phallus, splendidly erect, at last delivered from enchantment, O'Shea fretted, while in the cramped area she freed the skirt, dragged at her girdle, slid free. Pale, she lay back on the seat, and, caressing, he tuned her to readiness, passion streaking his loins, then, dismayed, felt her changed, hostile, slipping from him. 'What's wrong?' he gasped, fearful only of mistiming, spending himself in a too rapid assault, 'What is it?'

Stubborn, she still resisted.

He pulled back.

'Can't,' she whimpered, dishevelled, 'Not in the back of a car, Brendan, the first time we make love . . . I just can't.'

At that moment the overflow, the collapse.

They dressed.

He turned the car from the tide, the shrieking birds, and drove inland, the sea black as the light fell.

'Do we have to stay the night?' she ventured.

They had been motoring for at least an hour, O'Shea at the wheel like a man glad he has been wronged, Noreen alongside, mutely culpable.

'Yes.'

'Couldn't we go home?'

'No, we could not.'

'But The Castle's what's wrong, on the beach you were'—

'We are going back to The Castle for the night.'

The tone was unanswerable, and in the tone, the cut of him over the wheel, she recognized that he was at the same time punishing her, and—freshly secure—challenging The Castle. Instantly and uneasily, she was reminded of that moment in the bar at Athlone on Saturday, the barman's—'All before you now'—and his bland response, followed by the stripping of disguise, as she saw it, the male in him, stark, confronting her. She shut up for a while, pondered the darkness descending the mountains, thickening the valleys, then spoke again, a milder plea.

'Well, do we have to go back for dinner? Couldn't we have it on the way?'

He thought about this. Determined as he was to dare the bridal chamber—and conquer it—the idea of avoiding dinner in The Castle appealed. Last night was still grotesquely with him: Mulcahy rattling his testicles and the Manager presenting martinis for deeds not done. The memory might easily spoil his appetite.

'I suppose we could. For a change.'

In the next nightlit town they found the hotel—it catered mainly for the 'commercials'—and voted it tolerable. The dining-room décor was depressing (*café-au-lait* unpardonably piped with melon) and a kitchen odour hung about like a bad mood but the menu was fair and they were both lightened by the unaffected dullness of the place. As they waited for the soup, the tables around were deserted. Noreen watched him. He was frowning luxuriously, and her first impulse was to loose her temper, tear into him, and tell how incorrigibly selfish she thought he was. Curbing this, God only knew how or why, she travelled on to sympathy and from that to self-accusation. When she could no longer take his silence, she looked humbly for talk.

'I'm sorry about what happened, I'—

'Stop blaming yourself, it doesn't matter that much.'

'Blaming myself! I'm not blaming myself.'

'Why apologize then?'

'Because I was trying'—she groped—'I only wanted to'—

'Well, don't blame *me*, that's all.'

'Oh, damn you,' she struck back as the waitress mothered up with the bowls. Scenting gabble on her lips, O'Shea scowled the woman to silence. She left, offended.

The brown soup smouldered before them.

Then the arrival of the nuns brought distraction. A car pulled up outside, there was a butterfly commotion in the narrow hallway, and veils swaying, wimples bobbing, pleats fluttering, the four entered. The waitress hurried in to fuss, talk a welcome, and deferentially accommodate them in an alcove which gave the suggestion of privacy although they must, of course, be heard, and were—with an angled stretch —just in Noreen's vision. Voices wavered, twined and wove, explained. They had been at a sister convent for the day. Now on the way home, they were having a treat—dinner out. They had telephoned Mother Imelda, who said, Why? and they said, It's Sister Patricia's birthday, and Mother Imelda said, All right, girls, but be home by Compline. So here they were!

'Well, isn't that grand'—the waitress was slapping cups and saucers together—'And you came the right time, we have lamb this evening.'

'Lamb!' cried the nuns and their wimples frisked for joy, 'Lamb!' and their wimples frisked again.

The waitress went off, the chatter spurted, the hosanna

skirls of laughter, the strange collage of black and white, divertimento. Noreen was glad of the intrusion, hopeful that it would quell the storm racking them both, but *he* (now that he held what he considered the advantage) would not let up.

He was immediately availing of the nuns—they were, after all, *women*—to hit not–too–obliquely at her.

'Nuns! The damn county's full of them.'

She halted over the vegetables—'So? Haven't they a right to the life they choose?'—vehemently skivering one of the brussels sprouts.

'What are they afraid of? Hiding behind those walls?'

'You're impossible.'

'No'—he gestured neutrality with his cutlery, a trick which he knew goaded her—'No, I just think they're scared, that's all.'

She refused to continue the argument, and looking over his shoulder, gave her attention to the four. Soon they took identities. There was Gabriel who was fat and barrelled and laughed to her toes; Jarlath who was tall, a lady, and dimpled; Patricia who was young, beautiful, her face set in the veil and coif, oh, just beautiful, and there was little Monica who was nothing at all, wordless, plain, hardly there.

'Mint sauce, Jarlath, pass the mint sauce. Don't take it all now,' Gabriel cried, admonishing, and they all quivered in mirth.

'Potatoes, Sister Monica, come on now, have some, they'll make you wise!' and this time they lay back, wide sleeves trailing, gurgled and trilled.

But Noreen was watching Patricia, amazed, wondering who, who was it she was so poignantly reminded of, and at that moment a tilt of the dark lashes told her: Aileen Dempsey, now Sister Lourdes, her classmate in school, who—that final year—decided to enter the Order, and implored Noreen to take the veil also, implored, right up to the June examinations, and afterwards in that extraordinary run of letters during the summer.

'It's angelic, isn't it?' he mauled into the reverie.

'Oh, don't be so callous.'

'Callous?'

'Yes, callous.'

'What sweet will you have?' he dismissed the subject.

'I won't have sweet.'

'Coffee?'

'No, thank you.'

'Well, I'll have both—and stop pouting.'

She began to cry, sheltering hands to her face, the softest crying, hardly to be heard, unless you were beside her to catch the tiny breath-sounds gathering, growing incoherent as the tears flowed. He gaped, helpless. Just that soft crying, her shoulders part of it now, trembling or nearly, breath gulping against itself.

'Noreen, what's wrong?'

Reaching over he placed a hand on her arm but she disowned his pressure, it was no good, the tears must come, so penitent, he watched until after a few minutes she lowered her hands, showed the reddened eyes.

'What was it, Noreen, I'—

'It was nothing,' clearing the moist stains with a corner of the ravelled napkin—'Just stupid of me. Never mind. Will we go?'

Chastened, he paid the bill and they rose. Leaving, Noreen averted her eyes from the nuns. Had they noticed? Had Patricia, the young nun who was beautiful, noticed? She didn't dare to look. While they got their coats on the hallstand, she listened. The same gaiety—and, even in a gap of silence, you could hear its barely suppressed beat.

There: the talk was free again. That was Jarlath, it *was* Jarlath—'But did you see Philomena? In the garden, on the sundial—and when Mother Veronica walked . . .'

The laughter broke, a farewell, still thinly with them beneath the lamp on the street outside as they got into the car.

Before they drove off, his mind a melange of wimples and slender voices and sobs, O'Shea felt, soothing, for her hand.

'Honest to God, Noreen, I'm sorry.'

She only nodded, smiled, but not her damp eyes.

En route to The Castle, weakened by that rising of her grief, he almost said—'Right, let's go home'—but yet didn't. Then when they drove up the avenue, and the building faced them, floodlit in the beams of a couple of waiting cars, he paused again: the mullioned lighted windows, the turrets, the towers, the moon hung above as if on wizard gantries hired for the night, the sky dusted clean and carnival starred—all the pursuing theatricality of the place was concentrated, and it sickened him. Not moving from the car, he glanced at her. She was staring at the porch. Some people were coming out on the steps. They recognized the Manager, priestly in pose, and with him a young couple, unmistakably a fresh honeymoon pair. O'Shea winced and beside him sensed Noreen's start. Fixed, they watched. The Manager was all benediction. From the car they couldn't catch the words but bride and groom listened easily, adored each other, and Yes, they seemed to indicate as they looked about, it is good for us to be here. The Manager was still suavely talking. A horror, a weird repulsion, an impulse to stop the show came at O'Shea like quick jabs, viciously. He heard—or thought he heard—her heart tripping protest beside him. They saw the Manager escort the couple—libatory arms semicircling them—back inside and towards the lounge.

Their shocked glances met—'You wait here,' he told her.

He entered by a side-door and hurried upstairs. While he packed recklessly, the room taunted him, fire, roses and rolled back sheets. Julia at her games again.

The luggage readied, he went down to pay the bill. The receptionist looked oddly at him—'I thought you'd be with us until tomorrow, Mr. O'Shea.'

'An emergency,' he rapped.

'Your cases—I'll ring for the porter.'

'No, please'—he restrained her—'It's quite light, I can manage.' The force of those hyperthyroid eyes, at this moment, could maim him forever.

He hauled down the luggage, stowed it in the boot, tossed Noreen a coat, and they drove off.

It had taken ten minutes, seemed neatly unobtrusive, but as they crossed the bridge, The Imp appeared on the steps, waving a surprised good-bye, and from the second floor window a dustcloth bannered, behind it Julia's foaming breasts and collaborator's smile.

O'Shea put on speed.

Afterwards they had only a jumbled memory of that night drive back across Ireland. Did it take them four, five or six hours? They didn't know. Did they stop at any point? Impossible to say. Were the small towns busy or asleep? Had there been any small towns? A few things they could recall vividly: galoons of cloud streaming in a westerly wind, unfathomably encouraging; from trees, lined or solitary, along the way, the leaves falling in serried flights; the plain, flat healing acres quizzing the unreliable hills.

The night was well wasted when they reached home—outside Dublin, on a still road, a house as ordinary as stucco and a box design could make it, but behind its boundary wall, between its pitted hedges, mad with sanity. The uncurtained windows sparkled. Near the front door a slow Virginia creeper tokened wonders. Off to one side, a rusty cypress shone like bronze.

With a discovering throb, Noreen thought of the first time she'd looked at the house, wanted it. That evening she had seen in a window children's faces, the flit of faces, instant and fugitive as dreams—

'Come on.'

He unlocked the door, carried her in, kissed her blindly. Switching on lights, they ran about the empty rooms. Furniture was piled untidy in the hall. Noisily they clattered upstairs. More empty rooms, the echoes of their footsteps filling them splendidly. Somewhere a window with a broken latch spanked the breeze. They found their bedroom.

The Dogs of Fionn

Eyes on some high ditch she'd flown yesterday on the heels of the hounds, enter The Lady of The Manor. The scatter of customers parted—baggy matrons, a snuff-coloured pensioner, two or three youngsters—and fell back as she stepped up to the counter.

'A hawf pound of hawm,' cried The Lady of The Manor.

If I was fresh to the village, I was still certain who it was. You don't mistake Cromwell's breed. Demeaned by solid ground, those well-shod feet fidgeted to find the stirrups again; the tweed skirt, thighs and rump betrothed to the saddle; square-chested, and, above, the long leathery features of the tribe.

'A hawf pound of hawm.'

Her brown fingers rained on the counter.

'Certainly, m'lady.'

Two young ones supported the shopkeeper as he hurried to serve. Ham, slicer, careful now—

'Wretched weathaw, Mallon.'

'Desperate, m'lady, desperate,' said Johnny Mallon, fussy over the slicer. *Whirrisssh, whirrissssh*, pink white-streaked slivers curled from the bone.

'Lot of fat there, Mallon'—

Panic.

'Sorry, m'lady'—Johnny jumped to it, switched the ham about, drove back his assistants, started again.

M'lady! Scrapings of the Ascendancy bucket and acting as if nothing had changed for the last three hundred years. The customers hung there, blurring as my astonishment thickened to humiliation.

'How's that now?'

'Bettah, Mallon.'

Johnny wrapped the purchase. I watched her. Straight-backed, eyes on another approaching ditch.

'Now, thank you very much.'

Handing over the ham, crouched for a pat on his shop-keeper poll.

She never saw him, never saw anybody as, flick of the reins, she turned and strode, rode from the shop.

Business picked up again, casually. Already, she'd crossed the footpath, and was sitting in her car. Before starting up, she glanced into the shop. From that cluttered dusk I raised a hand, one finger crooked. She saw my signal. She waited.

I don't think anyone noticed me leave. My eyes were on that Munnings' face behind the car window. She was lowering the glass. I stopped about a yard short of the car.

I'd no idea what I was going to say. She had bad eyebrows, stubby, smudged.

'Woman, a thought struck me.'

Pause. A hundred wars sabred between us.

'Yes?'

'All that,' I said, my tongue lithe metal, 'stopped about forty years ago.'

She gaped up at me, wheeled for an answer.

I turned away—'You should remember that.'

Her car rasped from the kerb, and sped off.

You read the history books, and they tell you—nothing. But now, walking down the street, I thought—my God, that's

why they went out to fight—because they'd ride you down.
And this is what it felt like, the clash, the aftermath . . .

Crossing the bridge on my way home, the oldest bridge in
Ireland, some said. Norman stone spliced at its layered
foundations. Bulging from late-summer rain, the river cut
noisily through four squat eyes below. I turned right, and up
the road which, topping the bluffs, sat on the southern bank.
A dash of sun. Opposite, a line of sallies held the light, rusting
it. Fragilely, the small leaves peeled and distributed fantastic
bloom.

Then, not far ahead, I saw a woman I knew by sight.
Young, fair-complexioned, with child, her face the opening
corolla of pregnancy, neat smock, slacks, sandals. I was thinking how well she carried her child—when the barrage of
whistles and catcalls and semi-articulated jeers struck, and she
faltered. Embarrassed, she looked at me, bravely came on.

We both guessed, almost instantly, the source. I could look.
Across the river, up the grey windowed wall of that sometime
workhouse which served now as a boot-factory. In the far top
line of windows anonymous heads bobbed. The jeering
started afresh, with more relish this time, savouring the target
—'Whittoo. . . . Any chance, Mrs. . . . night . . . Yeeippeee. . . .
Give us a . . . Hi, Ma'am . . . How's your . . . Psst . . .'—
spurting down, livid on the breeze. My blood spat. Must be
my day for war. She was beside me.

'I'm—sorry, I'—

My apologies failed. She stood there, her back to the river.
Hands pathetically shielding, she said something but another
burst spewing from above took her words. And decided me.

'I'll be back'—

Turning, half-running, I back-tracked, and recrossed the
bridge. They were moving fast too. The jeering had stopped.

The distant windows showed blank, inoffensive. The possibility that—nameless—they could escape with such facility rowelled me. Veering left, hurrying under the massive walls, I could hear—sieved by stone—the machines. I came to the great arched gateway, and entered.

ENQUIRIES . . .

In the small office, the air was mucilage. At the table-desk in front of me, a thin girl idled over a typewriter.

'May I see The Manager?'

'Of course, sir.'

Curiously registering the impetus about me, she took my name, and, within seconds, The Manager appeared. Confronted by the office, I'd experienced a premonition of dismay, and now, echoing that, his presence dented something in me. Still, my complaint rushed out. When I was through, he spoke civilly.

'Damned glad you came round,' he said—the accent, his red pavilion-cheery moustached face no lie, was Yorkshire. 'Fact is we've had a lot of trouble with them. Rough crowd mostly, I'm afraid. This gives me a chance. I'll take care of them for you.'

'Thank you'—

I'd have gone then, but it was too late. The rictus of camaraderie on his big face loosened for one second, purred sympathy, set stiff again.

Next, companionably gabbing, he was guiding me to the door. Together, we stood outside. The flagged yard, pale, sloped down from us to the jail façade of the main building. At our appearance, heads ducked in the high windows. We must meet for a drink sometime, was he saying? Looking up at the windows, he buttoned his jacket, slapped me on the shoulder, and moved off across the yard, his supple hand-made shoes swingeing the stones.

Willy Wynne, Con Moto

When *The Lyric* was built in the early 'forties, it was fashionable for a time to go there at least once a week. The 'best' people, the Parish Priest, the doctors, the solicitors, the Garda Superintendent, well-to-do shopkeepers (include wives, *embonpoint* and featly girdled, in all cases above except the initial one) inhabited the carmine plush area at the rear. They were, collectively, the 1/8s. Next, dun and not so plush, the 1/3s: those who were progressing, factory operatives doing well on overtime, shophands able to put by a bit, a variety of clerks, mechanics, and a few restrained couples saving their pennies and their passion for the day when. Beyond these, on wooden benches, and right to the *Modigliani* angles below the screen, the rabble hived, the 9*d*s: direct labourers, rags-bottles-and-bones men, demireps, idlers, simpletons, that echelon which had not yet shuffled off the workhouse past—inheritance rarely spoken of precisely because its suppurating reality was so hard to deny.

There was, of course, a degree of infiltration—but minor. Occasionally, some clerk, exulting in a festal bonus, invaded the 1/8s, received the murky rebuffs of the *élite*. Or one of the rabble might advance to the intermediate zone, there to sit—brassy reminder that it was a slithery world, that, neutrality or no, Europe's rumble-tumble might easily be here in the morning, and then what? Such anomalies only emphasized that *The Lyric* was an arena in which social divisions were jaggedly defined. Yet, in *The Lyric*, more than anwhere else, these same divisions were open invitingly to attack.

The night on which this was most memorably demonstrated was an—otherwise—ordinary night at the cinema. There was a fair attendance except for the 9*d*s., it was Thursday and the week's expenditure had diminished patrons in that area so that the corral geometry of the benches enclosed no more than half a dozen people. The programme scheduled was pleasantly humdrum. Without mishap, it unreeled to a Travel Feature (pre-war, cheap), regular interlude item between the 'short' and the main offering. As always, this was a sunny presentation, Mediterranean or Caribbean, enhanced by tawny beings who trod the littoral as if they had just emerged, full-formed, from the fluid ivory-yellow sand. For variety, the cameras sometimes moved inland to ramble the mountains, approving —with a *schwarmerei* that barely escaped self-parody—the 'quaint' and the 'timeless.' The effect was to introduce a well-being quite unadulterated by yearning, since these havens had for the moment—the panzers, the U-boats—been translated to the regions of the purely mythical.

The camera had, in fact, taken to the mountains—*The Lyric*'s masked sidelights contributing a melon hush of comfort, tobacco smoke hanging like an abstract of 'Relaxation'— when the background music picked on a tune familiar to everybody—*The Donkey Serenade*. If it was familiar to all, it was particularly the possession of the 1/8s. The piece had *ton* —part rhythm and part the macaronic flavour of the ditty, was distinct from the rag-bag traffic of the day. Further, it was aureoled by the courtly gesturing of Nelson Eddy and Jeanette McDonald, and thus gained an orphic beat. The 1/3s were in touch also but in a ruminant sort of way. Because their radios chanted eighteen hours of the twenty-four, the 9*d*s knew it well. They could be expected to revere it or shit on it according to their humour.

As the opening bars flicked off the sound-track, there was a susurrus of pleasure, succeeded by an impulse to join in, lilting, humming, any accompaniment but some, *some*: then— shift of feeling almost audible—the impulse was choked. Good breeding won. You didn't lilt or hum or whistle in these circumstances, you contained yourself, listened, allowed others to enjoy. Even the 9ds behaved ... *Dum-tee, dum-tee dee-dum, dum-tee, dum-tee, dum-dum* . . . Euphoria. *Mezzo-piano*. Mrs. Cyril McGovern, wife to the State Solicitor for the county, tapped her foot noiselessly and smiled. The mountains. The quaint village. Old man, jennet, pannier . . . *Dum-tee, dum-tee dee-dum dum-tee, dum-dee, dum-dum* . . . Someone commenced to whistle. Bold liquid warbling that made the orchestra its servant on the spot, captured the melody, and capered on.

Susurrus again. No. Crepitation. Quick check in the mobile gloom to place the sound. It seemed to be coming from the 1/8s, left-hand side, middle. It was. Who? Knees propped, the *artiste* was humped down in his seat, just the head visible, blonde gipsy sheen, and the face, tilted, smoothly intent, highly manipulable lips purring with the sphincter leger-demain of your born *siffleur*. So it's you, said the 1/8s, averting from the smart of recognition. Willy Wynne, *con moto*, continued whistling.

The Wynnes lived in a street which hung raffishly off the bourgeois trunk of the town. They sold fruit all the time, and herrings now and then. The door of the small house was constantly open. A barrow stood by the footpath. Hurrying between house and barrow, you carried away the patchouli of orchards, grubby orchards, and a sourly teeming sea. The mother was a big woman, unrepentantly zigane, the father a whiny runt forever bossed by the barrow. The sons and daughters were worn freckled specimens, banana-skin in pigment and psychology. Willy was nineteen.

Whistling. The opening strategy of the 1/8s was forecastable. No great philosophical insight was needed to tell them that if they didn't hear the whistling, then, in some sense, it ceased to be. They decided not to hear, entrenched instantly on this ground, and waited. The 1/3s were amused but uninvolved, the 9*d*s unconcerned: Rose Hand, dozing in a corner; the two wrinkled Tinleys, jockey-crouched, brooding on the afternoons' treacheries at The Curragh; three kids coughing over cigarettes. Indulging in a series of chromatic flourishes, vibrant and fluty, Willy led the orchestra into the primary theme ... *Twee-twee-twee, twee-twee-twee, tu-reep tree ...*

An extraordinarily dogged of brief tussle followed. The communal spirit of the 1/8s fought by every shift and deceit imaginable to deny the sound. They gave themselves to the screen, they gave themselves to fantasies of lust and profit, they adventured, pot-holing among caves of thought and feeling they rarely visited. And for a space it seemed possible they would win. Until Vin Tierney, grocer cantankerous, sclerotic, broke ranks—the Wynne's owed him £75—and let fly a phosphorescent dart of hostility in Willy's direction. That was it. One by one, then all at once, the 1/8s succumbed. No longer any question: Willy Wynne, gay *caballero*, was whistling.

The whistling, if you could be objective about it, *had* something winning—a fresh *toccata* exuberance which derived, in fact, from the ten-and-sixpence Willy had won at pitch-and-toss earlier in the evening. Further, the acoustics of *The Lyric*, usually recalcitrant, seemed to delight in the unexpected sound. Roof and walls took it in flight, put a shine on, let it loose again. *Toccata* it flew. Innocent in a way. So it might have remained—had not Willy's capillaries interpreted accurately, and at speed, the mood of his immediate audience. He looked about him, and confirmed. Minutely, the whistling altered.

Meanwhile, the 1/8s, recovering from the shock and propelled by a vehemence which surprised them, were binding to an opposition. As they joined, there was still the infantile shrugging hope that this might not have to be suffered after all... *Sweet-sweet-sweet, too-eee-too, tweet* ... No, apparently, it must. Traveller on the listening faces now a *risus* flicker that boded trouble. Do you mind, Mister Wynne? We'd prefer the orchestra unaccompanied. Ascending chiruppy cadences. *Pup.* So you can whistle! A run of trills pinked and pinged, frolic of self-discovery, accomplishment, and (oh, you bastard, Willy!) the lick of power.

He had, indeed, just glimpsed the delicate ferocity of the weapon he held. The natural *brio* of his beginning had early taken on the tinge of malice but the incipient, even premature, writhing of the enemy extended his vision dramatically. For an instant, he was Lenin. If his followers in the far benches were still dormant, the revolutionary lives with that —and Willy would. They'd come; the 1/3s didn't matter; the opposition were here. Luminous with exultation, he waltzed up the scale, inspected the field from high *C*, and then—no comment—glided to a prolonged, contemplative, and subtly teasing *A* ...

Either panicked by that or operating inside a rhythm which governs all such situations, the 1/8s made a common and debilitating blunder. Bob Geary of The Bank and one or two others had glanced back at Father Terry Walsh to see how he was taking it. Noting the glances, Father Terry hesitated, half-stood up, and glared, prognathous, unambiguous, at the offender. The adjacent rows quickly contributed supporting scowls. Mounted, however, from behind, and ameliorated by the dimness, the attack faltered, lost its way, ultimately grew ashamed of itself, and expired among match-boxes, cigarette-ends, and sweet-papers. Father Terry—thump of the seat—sat down.

Too-eee-twee, whit-too-eee, sweet-sweet-sweet-whit too-eee too-eee twee . . . What was to be done? Nobody knew. Skin wriggled as the silence built around a spiral of prickly twitters. No one looking at Willy. Came a low chuckle from the 1/3s, and it was left to Doc Markey—who had a tongue—to intro-duce the next stage. Beyond patience, 'Little shite,' said The Doc. Cinema-whisper. Willy paused as the 1/8s rallied, drop-ped a crotchet—rudely, and skittered after the tune again unsubdued.

War now, by God! The impact of The Doc's comment and Willy's reply was to clarify—and to blur. For a second, as if raised on a swivel-chair, the criminal was visible, and his malevolent intentions but, immediately, he disappeared in a visceral tangle which included Fair Day rows, St. Vincent de Paul, Jeanette McDonald, England, the cosy funnel of motes linking the projection-room and the screen, *graffiti* in certain parts of The Workhouse ruin, each item peculiarly vivid despite (or because of) this dusk which had spawned them all. And the slick of Willy's hair. Little shite.

Amigo mio, does she not have a dainty bray? They surveyed him again, eyes on all side snapping. Tilted face greased by the half-light, finicky spewing lips. Humping himself further into the seat, hands pocketed, legs crossed, God, wouldn't you love to give him one good—but there was a second marauder: the incorrigible safety of the brat. You could hardly clout him. Even threaten. Not here. Not anywhere. And well he knew it . . . *She listens carefully to each little tune you play* . . . Titters from the 1/3s.

Willy—measuring developments—could see Hubert Lynch, the Mrs., the two sonsy daughters, tearing at him, small dog's teeth sharp in the whites of their eyes. Grand. But it was time, wasn't it? his followers showed themselves. The mere wish was charismatic—

Tootle-tootle-tootle-tee

The 9ds were in! It was Rose Hand—*La Bella Senorita*—hers the contrapuntal support. The building seemed to shake itself, prepare for possibilities undreamt of; either in relief or apprehension the murk lightened, and Willy, elated, razzle-dazzled the melody through a narrowing bore, silver and intense. *Jasus*, this was marvellous—

'Do you mind?'

In this squeeze of agony for the 1/8s, Superintendent Paul Boyle was the man who dared. He was in the same row as Willy, four seats distant, no one between to dilute the arch-angel tolerance of the voice.

'Do you mind?'

Willy's head turned—eyelids drooping an immaculate synchronism—spouted a few metallic chirps into the Super-intendent's face, found its tranced jubilant slant again. *Accelerando* twirls. The Superintendent sat back in his seat, stared gaunt ahead. *Si, si, me muchachito!* Snapping eyes switched, bit blindly at the screen. Mountains, faraway village, old man, jennet, pannier.

Led by Rose, the 9ds had wheeled, and now sat poised, six surprised sailors manning the itchy guns of a new Potemkin. At their backs the screen mimed irrelevantly. Timid rustle through 1/3s. The 1/8s poisonously still. And, with the authority of one who has outstripped fallibility, Willy accepted the mandate. Feckless of the melody, the whistling abruptly soared so that the performer appeared to gain a position on one of the brute girders which braced the roof. That achieved, the spectacular piping was split by a scolding note, sub-song, modulated jeer that was blasphemously maintained.

The 1/8s winced—but kept control. Assuming the masochistic rigidity of the about-to-be-martyred, they watched the screen. That is, they watched what they could see of it because—events moving with the impetus of anarchy—the 9ds were already standing on the benches, gesticulating enthusiasm, and more clamorous by the second. Still, in gross concert, the 1/8s watched, endured that raucous untutored ballet, endured the insulting spew of sound from the inviolable girders, the murk above.

It was at this point the 1/3s wheeled, sober, imitative, but at once sucked into the rhythm of revolt. From aloft—slouched despotically in the seat, Willy could barely be seen—there was no let-up, the jeer more venomous. Above the rumpus, a shower was heard hitting the roof of *The Lyric*, running in sloppy waves on the resonant galvanize.

Who was first to the sequent image will never be known. Just before Rose shouted, Mona Coyle—the Poultry Instructress—found her left hand flipping to her face in a pathetically protective gesture. And there may have been others, anticipant and quailing. What Rose shouted into the excitement was—'*Piss on them, bhoy!*'

That many of the 1/3s had been suborned was indicated by the extra-loud roar which met the suggestion. The marmoreal fixity of the 1/8s spasmed, awesomely held. For the last time, the whistling altered. Instantly, Rose rapped her ranks to silence. Willy, continuing, no doubt, his search for low-slung comfort, had passed out of sight (one knee *did* show, a disconnected shine) but from the dark overhead the whistling came, flighted parabolically in the main yet with quirky variations, watery overtones, and, blooming in the slipstream, a cloacal breath that registered as the sportive after-thought of pure genius.

To their terrible stillness the 1/8s held. By the time The Manager arrived, it was all over.

The Fortune-Tellers

She started.

Going around the corner of Dawson Street—just as the bus took the turn into The Green—was Monica Harding. So Monica was back. Until she'd gone to London six months ago, Monica had been one of them, the group of six or seven who met nearly every Tuesday night in Katherine's place in Rathgar. Those evenings—the tea and the cigarettes and the talk. Talk of fashions, change a skirt, alter a dress, freshen a blouse, talk of lines on and lines off, engagements and weddings, the kidding, who's next for the jump, everybody knows, come on now, tell the truth . . . Was Monica back for good? She'd find out when they met—and they'd meet all right . . .

'Excuse me.'

She got off at the bottom of Harcourt Street. When she got in, Sheila was tidying, at the same time trying to curb the children. On the table were two apple-tarts and a gingercake. Friday evening, she remembered, Frank would be home. The talk was the usual—just talk.

'How were things at the office?'

'Oh, Helen left a note about Sunday.'

'Una said to call round tomorrow.'

Just talk until—she was wondering should she go up to her room, rest for a while—Sheila asked—

'Maura, would you ever mind those kids while I run down to Cassidy's for'—

'Can't Sheila, I'm going out right away.'

Sheila flinched—

'Doesn't matter. I can go later.'

So it was said. Slipping up to her room to change, she'd no regrets for having said it—she couldn't stand Friday evenings in the flat anyway—but the question was where? And on her own? Ring someone? Or Eithne? Madcap Eithne —funny how they got on together—from the city, young too, same age as Sheila, while she herself was country, quiet, easy-going. She hadn't seen that much of her since the announcement but Derek—the intended—was out of town and she might be game. Only a matter of crossing the street to find out. Right.

Washed and dressed, she threw on her raincoat again, coming down called good-night into the kitchen, heard Sheila's careless answer as she went out the door, and crossed to the shop. Eithne was at the counter, straw-coloured hair glossy, pale oval face shining, and getting slimmer every day.

'Eithne, let's go somewhere.'

Eithne looked startled, then—

'Sure, I'm game.'

Where? Anywhere. Pictures, theatre, a walk, see some of the girls, anything—

'Let's go to a fortune-teller.'

Thought from nowhere—but she'd hit it.

'God, yes'—Eithne—'You mean the one Betty and The Kinlens went to before Easter, what's-her-name, you know the one, above in Dorset Street, Gipsy Lee, isn't it?'

'Would you?'

'Be with you in two minutes. I've eaten. Have'—

'Not hungry.'

It was just on closing-time. They put up the shutters, locked the door, Eithne was ready in a flash, the two of them out a side door, and off to the bus stop.

'God, I'm glad you were free, Eithne.'

'Anything for a lark, y'know me.'

'It was such a day, didn't you feel it, I was'—

'Come on'—Eithne was watching the stop—'Run for it.'

They ran but the 'bus full' notice was up, and, when they'd waited ten minutes for another, Maura could no longer endure it—

'Let's go, Eithne. Taxi's on me.'

They got a taxi in The Green—and they were away.

'Dorset Street, please,' Maura called as the taximan slid back the panel.

'What number in Dorset Street, Miss?'

She and Eithne looked at each other.

'We're looking for Gipsy Lee's place—the fortune-teller's.'

'God bless the women, they can never know enough.'

'Well,' Eithne prodded, 'can you find her for us?'

As if sure of its destination, the taxi was pushing northwards through the traffic. Relaxed at the wheel, the taximan talked—

'Can I find her for you? I can find her all right but, if it's a fortune-teller you want, I can take you to a better one than Gipsy Lee. Gipsy Lee wouldn't carry drinks to the woman I'm thinking of.'

'You know a better one?'—Maura.

Well, he didn't exactly know this fortune-teller himself. The wife had got word about her from Peggy, a friend that called round maybe once a week. The woman was a marvel, show her the palm of your hand, and she came out with your past, present, and to come, same as if she was reading it out of a book. And no catch. She was no money-grabber. Not like the whipster over in Dorset Street—

'This woman has The Gift,' he concluded, 'there's no doubt about that.'

'We'll take her.'

The taximan—they'd both responded to him, fortyish, with 'the Irish emigrant's face' as Maura described it to herself—suggested they consult with the wife. The house was near and it was no trouble to call. She would have all the details.

Eithne chattered on and on—

'Anyway, a few of us decided why not? so off to Madame What's-this-it-was, Zelida, no, Zelinda, that was it, Madame Zelinda in The Fun-Palace, did I ever tell you this, she's an albino, to see her in there with the white hair and the pink eyes, you wouldn't believe it, Maura, but wait till you hear . . .'

Letting her ramble, Maura returned to her own reverie. Queer the twist a day could take, she was thinking. Her suggestion —out of the blue, and they'd picked *this* taximan, and he knew *this* particular fortune-teller, and then his willingness to help, seek her out, it was—

'Maura will you stop moping, we're not going to a wake.'

'Sorry,' she smiled, 'I've evenings like that.'

'Don't I know it.'

The laughter of old banter about them, they entered a *cul-de-sac* and pulled up at a kennel of a house, third from the end.

The taximan got out, went inside, and emerged followed by the wife, a big-bodied woman with a bold face. One foot on the running-board, she spoke to them through the window—

'I had that woman's address last week but I declare to God it went out of me head. All I know is she's from Templeogue. Go round as far as Peggy's place—he knows the house—in Eccles Street, and she'll give it to you. And, if you're hunting a fortune-teller, you'll find none better. She's a strange woman, it seems. Deaf, y'know, deaf as a beetle but she has The Gift all right . . .'

She looked in more closely at the girls, glance skipping slyly—
'She'll give you initials, and she'll do The Marriage-Bed with the cards too—for them that wants it that is.'

Lopsidedly, their laughter fell away.

'We don't take it too seriously'—Maura.

The wife breasted this—

'She was never far wrong yet. But go round to Peggy's anyway, and see what happens.'

Thanking her, they set out again. Eccles Street was beside them. They drove almost the length of it, and drew up outside a wasted Georgian house. The taximan left to search out Peggy. They waited anxiously as he rang. After a moment, the door opened and a wispy adolescent girl appeared. There was talk, the door closed on the wisp, and the taximan returned.

'Curse of hell on it'—the lean face morose—'Her one evening off.'

They studied the house-front.

'Couldn't they find her for us?'

'Not a hope,' he brooded by the taxi, then jerked alive, 'Never mind. We'll go up that far. The Guards in Templeogue might have word of her. We'll chance it.'

He noticed Maura's eyes swivel to the meter.

'Don't let that worry you. I'll treat you decent.'

As they hung over a decision, he made it for them, getting in, and turning the car.

'Templeogue,' sang Eithne, settling herself for a jaunt, 'here we come.'

Obstacles, and yet it was right, somehow, that they should have to *pursue* her, show their good faith—

'If it was only a matter of crossing the street, you wouldn't bother your head,' the taximan was saying, 'but when you have to search a thing out it's different entirely.'

They'd crossed the river again, and were climbing the slope on the south side.

'What's the betting, Maura?'—Eithne.

'We'll find her all right.'

'But would you believe a word she says?'

'Sometimes'—Maura hesitated—'it's strange the things they can tell.'

'Like the horoscope?'

Game they'd played, leafing through the magazines in the shop, the Horoscope Column, Single Girls Section, Eithne under *Capricorn*, she under *Virgo*, Eithne joking as they they turned the pages—'Now let's see what's in store for The Virgin!' She glanced down at her palm—there was something you couldn't dismiss so easily—and scanned its confusion: Marriage-line and Life-line, Line of Heart and Line of Destiny, broken lines, whole lines, angles and curves—

'That deafness she has,' the taximan came in, 'she's totally deaf, that's significant, they say.'

'How significant?'

'The Gift, you see,' said the taximan, 'is a sort of compensation—for the affliction, like.'

'Never any damn good,' he told them, 'unless they have something like that—something in the ailment line, that type o' thing.'

Evening that was meant then? The woman waiting too, knowing—in her way, prepared? It was believable. Entering the belt of new housing on the city fringe, they'd found the roads in a lull of quiet, and, captive to it, fallen silent. The roadlamps had just come on, yellow glare weird on the pavement, gardens washed to a filmy tinge, and, clouding all, a hush that had strayed from the small hours. A wooded park showed, and Maura caught the sound of a pigeon's call, deep among the trees. String to it, she strained to hear it again. It came, stronger this time, doubling, beat farewell as they moved on.

'Templeogue ahead,' came word from the front.

The two sat up as a stoutly gabled pub appeared in the distance with the air of a landmark.

'That's "The Nest" '—the taximan—'The Barracks is only a hundred yards beyond it.'

Passing "The Nest", they went on to the cement-faced Barracks. The taximan pulled up and got out.

'Say your prayers now,' he joked as he left them. A minute passed, he reappeared, was at the window.

'No luck'—again the long face—'but we'll try "The Nest", there's just the chance.'

He sat in and started the engine.

'No one inside know of her?'—Maura.

'Not a soul—but don't fret till we see how the ball hops down here.'

Calmly, he drove back to the pub.

'Take it easy for a second'—again he left them.

'Don't know about you,' Eithne commented, 'but I begin to smell wild goose romp.'

Watching the swing-doors of the pub, Maura said nothing.

'Anyway, if he finds her, he finds her, if he doesn't, so what? We just hop back to a picture in town. Did I tell you about Valerie Rogan?'

'No.'

'The bitch is supposed to be doing bridesmaid, and she hasn't put a foot near me yet to talk about the dresses. My bet is, remember I told you, Maura, she'll turn up in sackcloth. She's pathetic on clothes.'

The doors parted.

'Must be a hex on us'—he arrived back—in deeper mourning—'Not a word of her in there.'

'They're sure?'

They were sure.

'No one else we could try, I suppose?'—Eithne.

The taximan shoved back the peak of his cap, pulled his mouth apologetically, whorled the stubble on his chin—

'I'll tell you what we *could* do. There's a carnival over in Kimmage and there's bound to be a fortune-teller there. It's only a mile up the road, and when we're this far . . .'

They both looked at Maura.

'Some of them carnival fortune-tellers are not bad now'—the taximan.

Maura said nothing.

'Oh, come on, let's go, for the heck of it'—Eithne.

'Right'—the taximan got in.

They set out for Kimmage.

Reeling in a field off the road, the lights of The Carnival drew them. Coloured bulbs whirled brilliant scarves that flecked the taxi as it pulled up at the entrance, juke-box chords spanked the air, chairoplanes skirted and screamed, a merry-go-round wheeled, children's screeches tussled with shouted verdicts from the tents and stalls, and from a shooting-range near the gate came the bright spit-spit of air-guns.

A bushy-browed man, spilling out of a big overcoat, was selling tickets. At a gesture from the taximan, he approached.

'Would there be a fortune-teller within?'

The man looked casually into the taxi before replying.

'Divil the one. They're illegal now at carnivals.'

'Ah . . .'

'Illegal since last year. Some new law they brought in.'

'That's what we pay them for,' Eithne griped, 'Great.'

'Well, there's your law,' said the man, 'There's your law.'

'What the hell have they against fortune-tellers?'

'Damned if I know. Well—sorry—have to get back here. Good'—

'Wait—Maura stopped him—'Do you know any fortune-tellers around here?'

He gave them his slow stooping look again.

'Ever hear of one in Templeogue?' she prompted.

'You mean Mrs. Monks?' his face switched, 'Sure I know her. She's the best in Dublin.'

A wave of jubilation struck. The mad music of The Carnival abandoned the fairground, poured into the taxi, gulfed them in a wild crescendo, deafening them to everything except a single phrase—so that all the time the man by the front window appeared to be repeating, '*You mean Mrs. Monks, You mean Mrs. Monks You mean* . . .'

'Maura, you were right, you were right.'

'Had an idea we'd find her'—the taximan.

Determined, Maura was following up—

'Do you know her address?'

It seemed absurd that he could know, could snap his fingers, topple the wall—

'Her address?' He looked up the road, let his mind's eye ramble, summoned it back, looked in at them again—'Nash Road, it is . . . number seventy-four, I think. A few bends of the road will take you to it.'

He gave them a clutter of directions and returned to duty at the gate. Triumphantly, they turned back, and, hurrahing each other with smiles, made for Nash Road.

'There's Nash Avenue.'

They entered the avenue, darkly lit, and still.

'It's somewhere off this'—cruising until a name-plate showed, they swung left—'Nash Road.'

'Seventy-four, he said?'

'That's it.'

It was difficult to see the numbers even when the fanlights showed faintly against a light within. The taxi progressing speculatively, Maura let down the window and put her head out—

'Slow. Wait a minute . . . sixteen, eighteen, Eithne, you check the other side—no, stop, could we ask her?'

A woman was passing on the footpath.

'Excuse me,' the taxi slowing to a halt, Maura called her, 'we're looking for Mrs. Monk's place—the fortune-teller.'

The woman, aproned, stopped and came over, arms folded about a sag of bosom.

'We think it's seventy-four.'

'Tell me'—Eithne—'Is she really the best in Dublin?'

She looked troubled, clogged, as she took them, their questions, in.

'Yes'—she got out eventually—'a good woman surely.'

The folded arms gripped each other, closely shielding—

'I never had call to go to her,' she said, 'but any who did had a lot come true after. Only'—her lips pinched—'you've come too late, you see.'

Too late? Slipping back her cuff, Maura protested—

'It's only eight o'clock.'

'That's right,' the taximan examined a pocket-watch, 'Just eight I make it.'

'Oh, it's not that—not that at all.'

They waited.

'Poor Mrs. Monks, God rest her, is buried this fortnight.'

Maura stiffened, stared her. With a limp face, the taximan looked up: his hand slipped out and switched off the engine.

'You really mean she's dead?' Eithne asked.

The woman didn't answer.

After a moment, the taximan spoke—

'Thanks a lot anyway, ma'am.'

Then she moved away.

Bottom of Harcourt Street, the fare paid, Eithne—some excuse or other—bailed out.

'Bye, Maura. See you'—she was crossing the street to the side-door entrance.

'Bye, Eithne,' Maura waved, 'See you.'

Edging for a position, the taxi made it, nosed towards the lights.

She stood there, watching it go, saw it through the junction, into The Green. Crowds were out in The Green—she watched —footpath black on the College of Surgeons side, and black beneath the trees, and a maul of traffic between, cars, buses, scooters, cyclists, beyond them—shiver and blend, shiver and blend—the cream and crimson of the Grafton Street blaze.

Their Quiet Arena

'Who's that, I wonder?'

Sitting by the fire, lambskin a purr of warmth between them, the room fat with drapes and cushions, when the bell rang.

'See anyway, darling.'

Crossing cosy legs, she returned to the magazine on her lap.

He left the room and walked up the hall. The storm, banging and banging of a cage-door almost unhinged. Switching on the light, he could make out a shape caught in the reeded glass. Like a ruined snapshot it swam and blurred, wavered to nothing, milkily took form again. He opened the door. The storm leaped, swung a bright claw of rain the length of the porch.

'Good night.' The figure Paul saw on the top step might have been lofted there by the tide—'Can I do anything for you?'

Left shoulder wincing in the windspray, the fellow—very tall—looked, took back the look, paused. Thirty, maybe, bearded, brown beard, Christ or Roger Casement, face set and planed for a beard—

'Could you give me a cup of tea?'

Accentless.

'Come in.'

Quickly, Paul shut the door. In the hall, the stranger's long gaberdine, mulberry, buttoned to the throat, dripped on the tiles. The tan shoes, sodden and chapped, looked good quality.

'Hold on a minute there.'

He didn't take the offered seat. Stood by the hall-stand, head cricked from the light. So, if he didn't care to sit down —fair enough.

Delia perked when Paul re-entered—

'Some fellow passing,' he aimed his voice low, 'Don't know who he is—wants a cup of tea.'

She waited only a moment—

'Might as well give him something. Put on the kettle for me, will you?'

In the kitchen off the living-room he filled the electric kettle and threw the switch. Mulling. Unusual-looking customer. What had him loose on a night like this? Should he have left him alone out there? Nothing to steal, in any case, except the waxplant or a choice of missals. He went back in—Delia still reading, shins toasting—strolled out to the hall. Wouldn't have surprised him to find the guest gone, *dissolved*, but he was there, islanded on the same spot.

'We'll have it for you soon now.'

'Thank you.'

Downlooking. And no accent in the world. Try him with a cigarette and see what happens. It was refused with a shake of the head, an odd light shedding cover and commencing to lope in the nearly citrine eyes.

'Paul?'

'Excuse me a second.'

He went in.

'Why don't you bring him in to the fire? He must be drowned.'

'Should I?'—her chiding left him the task of trying to damn a fleck in the man's eyes—'I don't know—I'm not sure.'

'How not sure?'

'Look, just go and make the tea. I'll stay with him.'

He went back out.

This time the man was seated, the soaked gaberdine here stuck to the skin, there flapped in scarecrow folds. Ask him to take it off? In the background was the kettle-to-teapot gout of water but any following sounds were lost in the roar outside. The visitor continued to count the tiles. Nothing to say to his host—rather as if he considered it his right to be admitted. Paul spoke up—

'Bad night to be out.'

Nod. A hand pulled across the sallow forehead. The fingers came away brimming with water which—the hand dropped tiredly to the knee—melted into the dark cloth. Hands clasped now, shapely, unused.

'Travel far?'

'Yes.'

Looking at the door. All right. Leave if you like. Propping his ham against the hall-stand, Paul dragged out the cigarettes again, took one, and lit up.

'And where've you come from—if you don't mind my'—

'Cambridge.' One of the *learned*, maybe.

'And you're going to?'

'I'm going to Bristol.'

Via the wilds of Ireland.

'I see'—wishing Delia to hear, keep her in touch, Paul slewed the words—'You were working in Cambridge?'

'I was a mechanic'—glancing up, showing tough bones in the moist cheeks, eyebrows—jabs—which stopped before they started—'I worked at machines.'

'That tea should be ready,' Paul topped the cigarette, 'I'll get it for you now.'

He walked down the hall but once into the living-room—

117

the carpet to dull his steps—sped. Delia, beside the cooker, fluttered when she saw him.

'Look,' he led her out to the scullery, opened the back door a few inches, 'You stay here.'

'What'—her breath tangled—'What's he'—

'Listen to me. I'll keep near the front door. If anything goes wrong, I shout. All you have to do is leave—and the same for me. He can have anything he wants in the house—if he wants anything. Is the tea ready?' He'd almost forgotten. 'Right.' His hand on her arm wilting to a cinema *cliché*, he stepped into the kitchen, took up the tray, put it down again.

'Delia,' he went back, held her firmly, 'I'm only taking precautions. It may be nothing at all.'

'Okay.'

'Good.'

He released her, left, took up the tray again.

'But,' she said, 'you shouldn't have let him in.'

Surprise.

Standing right on the lambskin was the man, clothes still dripping, tufts of steam saluting the heat of the fire.

'Thank you.'

Paul—saying nothing—left the tray on a pouffe beside Delia's chair, and moved off to a point near the door which led into the hall. The man showed no interest in—anything. Behind him, the terra-cotta of the fireplace was thinly lacquered with vapour.

Now what?

Jerkily, he got to work above the tray. Paul watched— spout's gurgle, clinking, creamer tilted over the cup—drawing some ease from the normality of the operation.

'Paul?'

'Yes?'

Gulping, the guest paused.

'If you want more tea—I can make it.'

'Right.'

Resumed gulping.

'You've somewhere to stay tonight?' Paul—to cut out the sound, 'Or are you just . . . going on?'

'There's always somewhere.'

Swigging the tea, golloping the biscuits.

'Always somewhere.'

Crunch-scrunch.

One biscuit left.

For God's sake, don't eat like that.

The tea finished, cup and saucer clinking on the tray.

He's going.

Crossing swiftly, he passed Paul. A muggy odour hung behind. Paul followed him out. On the back of the gaberdine piebald splotches of drying.

'Good night'—spoken to the door as he slipped the catch, went out, leaving it wide. Rain on the steps, the unsteady lunge of the wind giving it a vicious fall. The visitor walked down, straight into the sheen of it, gone.

A blast whirling through the house slammed the door. The back. He ran. She was there. First, he closed and bolted the scullery door.

'Relax now'—he took her in his arms—'He's gone. It's okay.'

He brought her inside, settled her in the arm-chair, threw on more coal.

'Shot of whiskey's what we want,' he decided.

They had the drink.

'Well, how's that feel?'

'Not so bad.'

'You look'—he went over, took her hands—'I'll get you a rug.'

He ran upstairs for a couple of rugs, came down, shawled her.

'That better?'

'Thanks.' She dragged her chair nearer the fire. 'I'll be all right.'

He had another drink.

'Paul?'

He glanced up.

'What did he look like?'

'Oh—you didn't see him'—he delayed—'Delia, shouldn't we let it drop?'

'No—I want to know.'

He tried to go over it—he was tall, with a beard, and it wasn't that he looked *dangerous*, really, except for the eyes, sometimes, and the way he ate, that made you . . .

Bristly silence. Smoothed only by the storm's removed noise, and flames teasing the bars of the grate.

'Paul?'

She pointed to the lambskin.

Dead-centre on the white spread of wool was a circle, a spoor, of damp. It was there, often feinting to vanish in the thick curls but—live as light—or shadow—quickly, insistently, returning to display itself.

'It'll dry out.'

Twisting from her face, he set the rug against the pouffe in front of the fire.

They went to bed.

From the landing—'Please, Paul'—she sent him back to check the doors and windows.

They were under the blankets, lights out, when she felt for his arm—

'Paul?'
'Yes.'
'Paul, that man, did you actually'—
'Yes, Delia, I did.'
'You're sure, Paul?'
'Quite sure.'

Gates

About four o'clock, rounding the bend beside the house, he saw Chrissy's car. Light astigmatic on the bonnet and windscreen, swinging across and slowing to park. At once, he swerved into a mock collision, pulled up inches from her car's bumper. When he looked, she was already getting out and making for the small gate, pushing a way through the fug of summer heat.

Seemed she was in a hurry. He stepped out and slammed the car-door, heard that noise clout the quiet, announce the male, the hunter, returned from quotidian safari. Then he saw Mary, and the house's scrabble of panic came awkwardly to meet him. She was standing there beyond the gate, fingers groping for some hold on the flimsy topshoots of the beech hedge. Chrissy reached her. He ran—

'What happened?'

'Get her in first, come on.'

They helped her across the strip of grass. She hadn't said a thing, simply gave herself, passive and drawn. His abrupt thought was that fright had stolen from him, left instead of his wife-bride someone who was Not-Mary. Wearily between them, she took the steps and they went inside. The hall was cool but tacky cool. Wrought iron shadows watched them pass to the living-room—

'Careful now . . .'

They got her on the sofa. She lay there, child-frail, her colour wavering white above the tartan blouse.

'Brandy,' Chrissy demanded.

'In the kitchen cabinet—over the sink.'

She went out.

'Are you sick—what is it—what'—

He took a yielding hand as she looked up, recognition steadying between them. Then, a queasy moue, she rode a shiver, recovered—

'He went up the road.'

'Who?'

Her eyes found the window, retreated, bemused—

'The man.'

The brandy. He watched while she sipped from the slanted glass. Flaccid against the brim, her lips worked slowly. Above, Chrissy's bony sideface. The man. An entering quiver of the garden added its signal, repetitive, vindictive, monotone. On the prop of an elbow she sat up, rubbed her nose in an infant gesture of exhaustion—knowing, perhaps, it would ease them —finished the brandy, shook her head as if to scatter vertigo, and turned to their concern.

'What was it?' Kneeling, he took her hands.

'He was here twenty minutes, I kept him off, grabbed the old poker'—she stopped—'got outside on the road, he ran'—

'She phoned me,' Chrissy cut in, 'Langan, I know him, he was running, lives in one of the cottages up the road there, long, red-faced'—she looked for Mary to confirm—'It was, wasn't it?'

Recoiling, she nodded.

'Did he touch you?'

'He tried'—she turned towards the wall where foliage shadows swayed, pinnate, meshed—'I'd have killed him.'

Her appearance still suggested fright, fright subdued but

ready at pleasure to rise and course again past all the beaten doors of her security. That, and her leaning glance, provoked in him a ruck of feral excitement. He felt Chrissy's seconding urge, moved for the door—'I'll get him.'

'You'll know,' Chrissy called, 'a roll of paper under his arm, you can't miss'—

'Right'

He didn't look back. 'I'd have killed him,' she was saying to the other's 'Easy now, rest yourself' as he went outside.

Half a minute took him to the row of cottages, and he slowed the car. A dozen in all, squat, scabby, queerly gabled, crude pelmets above the porches. He drove past the gardens, sour patches caught between the cobbles and the road. One (he remembered) did aspire to style, and in an odd key spoke for the others. There it was, the fronting hedge, blackthorn, from which several birds reared to strut in unkempt topiary.

That was at the seventh cottage. In the doorway of the ninth, he saw the man. Long, yes, put him at forty, forty-five, capped, the face not red but mallowy, a tout's face. He stopped the car, got out, and at a run crossed the road. Woman also in the doorway. Her house probably—he'd delayed to gossip, had that look. Or that pretence. They watched him come—

'You bastard,' he hurled it.

Surprised, the woman was backing away. As he threw open the gate, belligerence began to find its balance on the mallowy face—

'Mind your tongue'—tone of one not to be wronged—'There's a witness at my elbow.'

He made for the man—

'Christ, if you've harmed her'—

'Who?'

'My wife.'

'I never touched your wife.'

'You were seen, damn you.'

'They're liars then—don't you know me?' Stench of sweat and porter. 'Joe Langan. Who told you'—

'Stop it, I tell you I *know*, I *know*.'

'Don't blow up on me now. We can talk—without shouts.'

'I was in. I admit that'—shifting the roll of paper from right to left—'but it was you I wanted.'

'Don't lie to me.'

'Work. I dropped in looking for a job.'

'He's right,' the woman edged forward—curl of moustache, subfusc caution about the eyes, 'He told me, looking for work, that's what he said.'

'Someone mentioned to me,' the man commenced to elaborate, 'one of the boys, maybe, you wanted help for the garden, so I called to see.'

'I don't employ anyone in the garden.'

'Out of work he is'—the woman shot back—'these six months.'

'Just a few hours labour. And—you not there—the wife gets upset.'

In the next doorway, an old man appeared.

'Not much good being idle'—her wearing whine.

'He attacked my wife.'

'Women new to a place get frightened easy,' the woman again, 'I seen it often when they're new, I mean, if a stranger appears at all . . .'

The old man spat, hiss against the heat. Antiphonal and slippery, they kept it up—

'Happened last year, same bloody thing. Phil Connors accused in the wrong by that new doctor's wife.'

'Never heard the like said of Joe Langan, not in my time I didn't.'

'Jasus Christ of Almighty, I wouldn't lay a finger on a child.'

'Nor any Langan here or hereabouts—and I knew them all.'

No stopping them, and—the sentences weaving bolder—on it went until, sick of it, he was turning away, making for the car. Instantly, the man was in pursuit—

'Wait. Here, don't go like that, hold on a minute'—

'I don't want hard feelings. If I scared her, I'm sorry, you know that . . .'

At the gate, his arm was taken—

'Christ, I apologized, didn't I, I wouldn't harm the woman.'

Tugging free, he made no reply but, stubborn, the man followed him to the car—dangerously on the crown of the road where his rage had abandoned it.

'I'll write her a letter. Will that do you then? Well?'

About to open the door, he was offered a long dirty hand—

'Come on. Shake on it. Come on.'

Refusing, he tried to escape but the man closed, and the handclasp joined them.

'That's more like it, no hard feelings—and, for any misunderstanding, you know . . .'

Releasing his hand, he got in, and pulled the door shut.

'Good luck now'—the man waved.

He drove ten yards up to turn. Coming back, he saw the woman, watching yet. The old man had gone in. And, from the margin, the other saluted, a smile lying close to his mouth—

'Good luck, sir.'

Hands watery on the wheel, he headed home.

'Jim?'

He paused in the hall.

'Jim?'

He went in. Looking better, she was still on the sofa,

'What happened? You're all right?'

'Chrissy?'

'In the kitchen. Are you all right?'

Solfege climb in the vowels.

'I'm all right.'

He crossed the room, and sat down by the fireplace.

'Well—did you—find him?'

The room narrowed, pleated, for discovery. Her expression puckered—the same motion, could have been.

'He'—glance switching to the window—'said he was just enquiring for a job.'

When he made himself look back, her face was from him.

'I didn't—I shouldn't have listened to him but'—

He could see her shoulders, the light curved span, and, under the taut blouse, arc on ribbed arc suppling to the waist. On the wall, the foliage shadow frivoled echoes.

That night, when the man came by with more apologies, explanations, he—saying nothing this time—showed him the road. A thin advance—and comfortless. For that moment, simply, it must serve.

Exposure

Midnight, the hurry home, home Joan and don't spare the . . . suddenly the skid, and she was slicing, whipslew, off the road, *smack*, splintering the crutchy paling, and shooting—the wheels four spick blades—from the low bank into a broad pool beyond the reel and dip of the windscreen. Then, nothing remembered, at a guess the interval was three, four, minutes, until she came to, threads of blood wet on her forehead, the car still afloat.

Jesus

She didn't move her lips but every vein, pore, duct, articulated terror inside the two shut syllables. All over her, instant, as though for this tocsin it had bided years, sweat broke and ran. She gripped the steering-wheel, perhaps a jerk of hope that she could brake the spin of happenings, even work, strain it backward to the ordered motion of safety.

The car was sinking. Submerged, the headlamps funnelled twin beams, mildly bobbing. The water was stained brown, its boggy tint evident in the incongruous splay of light. She glanced out, searching. The place was deserted, no houses, no traffic on the road. On the other bank a path. Lifeless also. The car was boxing her, the river susurrus through joints and corners, lap-lapping her ankles. She tried again, and in spastic fury began to struggle with the door. No good. The window. Scrabbling, she lowered it. Raw, clinging air entered. Ditching her coat and shoes—one splashed softly beside the handbrake—she levered, pushed, squirmed through, and the water struck, shocking her alert as she hadn't been since the ice tricked her.

Woollen dress, slip, bra, girdle, everything bandaged her in numb folds. She floundered towards a line of elms, black candlabra, swaying near, vanishing. The bank was nowhere. She went under, surfaced, shuddering at the turf-taste. Drowning, she thrashed and clutched for the branches swinging down. She'd begun to scream, feet still beating for the bottom, the elms thinning, gone, no, from the trees, something—a hand. In a rigor of screaming she flung her arm, hand. Someone held, strong, and—the river yielding, sliding back into itself—pulled her against the bank, on to the crusted mud.

Of course, it was a story to dine out on for years, all that, and then, how, shivering, she'd been transferred to a passing car (tartan rug fortuitously ready on the back seat) and taken to hospital. Calm, sodden, what she remembered most from the journey was the halitosis presence of the river, so dominant, so much *her* possession, that she wriggled in humiliation. At the hospital they treated her for that ailment, boundless and penumbral, known in stethoscope journalese as 'shock'. And, it was decided, she would not be discharged for a couple of days.

By that evening, the affair was becoming enjoyable. The morning papers had carried the news. Telegrams and flowers and friends were collecting. She'd had the children shipped off to Moira, her sister, for a week, and left to her audience—the flankers, sororal and loyal, gained in the years since John's death—she shone.

'Joan, what happened? Who was the fellow? How'd it look —death's door? Were you terrified? Where's the gallant hero? Who'—

Always it came back to *him*. Who was he? She had no idea.
Did the man who owned the car know? She'd enquired: he
didn't. Nobody knew. She'd seen his face—behind the hand,
coming out of the elms—but couldn't remember it.

'He'll have to be found, we just can't let him disappear,'
Peggy Nolan, indignant, laid it down.

Was he big? Handsome? Would you say he was educated?
Wealthy?

Very likely he was all of those things—but she couldn't
say . . .

'I know, I can see him'—Maude Doyle took over, Maude
with her moods (the name, of course, was responsible) damply
oscillating between Tennyson and early Yeats—'A barrister
—taking a midnight walk by the river—brooding on his latest
brief, his hair is actor-grey and he's sadly handsome like, say,
Parnell!'

Vera Duffy, who aspired to second sight, announced that
it wouldn't surprise her in the least if the man eventually
married Joan.

'Don't laugh, girls, I've a feeling . . . just you wait . . .'

Gawky on the fringe, the nurses giggled, and straightened
their nunnish cuffs.

Joking aside, she did want to locate him. Curiosity, yes, and,
naturally, she wished to say, 'Thank you.' But to find him?
A newspaper notice seemed too, too what? Too ostentatious,
too organised. She could, perhaps, drive out to the spot
sometime and enquire. But that was—the thought aroused a
visceral confusion she couldn't explain. She put away the
notion. Her friends were keeping an eye out. Somebody
would discover him. Next thing she was leaving hospital, he
hadn't turned up, and she let it slide.

Now, exactly two months later, he had appeared. There he

was, sitting across from her, presentable enough, not unlike-able.

'Have a cigarette, won't you?'

He would. Limber in a sports-jacket and twills, he was the right side of forty, seemed well off—she couldn't be sure, you never could be nowadays. The shoes were unkept but that proved nothing. The lighter, the ash-trays, the first long in-haling—

'I'm delighted you called,' she said eventually, sitting down, 'We've all been wondering—just who you were.'

('Gaffney, Jim,' he'd announced on the doorstep, 'We met —at the river.')

She stooped by the fender to fuss over the fire—

'We searched everywhere'—glancing up into the open-air face: flat in its contours, scooped more than carved, under the neat head of nondescript hair: light, brown eyes met hers briefly—'but there wasn't a trace of you.'

As if ticking off everything she'd said so far, he nodded, drew on the cigarette. Then he looked around the room, her furniture—Danish, the shelved books, the Japanese statuettes above, the paintings and drawings—nothing too *dèclassè*, nothing too clamorously *avant-garde*, the carpet, the scatter of rugs, it was her best room. He took it all in, came back to the rug at the fireplace, shifted his feet, tapped a tip of ash into the tray at his elbow, and told her that he'd been meaning to call.

'And, I've been wanting to thank you—ever since that night really.'

Listening, he viewed his hand. Palm down, it rested on the chair's arm.

'Now that you're here,' she continued, 'I hardly know what to say.'

She stopped, wanted to drop the subject, offer him a drink, bring in coffee—

'All I know is you saved my life, and, well'—

She was looking to him for a concluding phrase but he didn't supply it, so, bridging the pause, she gave a lead—

'And you—I mean, how were you afterwards? You must have been'—

'I was all right,' he shrugged, 'I managed.'

'But you must have been frozen, drenched. That night—the cold is in my bones yet.'

Another shrug. The slightest change of posture seemed to bring him nearer the heat of the fire.

'Was—is—your home close to the spot? Had you far to go then?'

'No, not far. Half-mile up.'

His eyes, an unconscious response maybe, skimmed the room again, and she half-wondered if he could possibly belong to one of the toad-stool cottages which sat on the bluffs.

'Were you walking or'—she battled on—'It was such incredible luck for me you happened to be there.'

'I was just going home.'

'Oh . . .'

'I rang the hospital,' he said, 'three or four times.'

'You rang?'—that *had* surprised her—'Thank you, it was awfully kind, you really'—

'Trunk-calls,' he fiddled with the cigarette, 'I was down the country.'

'But, my God, the expense'—she was disconcerted—'Honestly, I think I had all the comforts. There you were, out doing your work, probably with a bad cold, and'—

'Bit of a chill.'

His face upset her, that second, it veered, too much veer in it, and, still, poised.

'The suit was ruined,' he said, crossing his legs.

'The suit'—her regret was immediate—'I never thought—

132

but that's wretched. Well, I'll simply get you a new one. You must let me, I *insist* on that, I want to, please.'

In a flurry, an earnest of goodwill, she rose to get him a drink but no, no, thank you. She sat down.

'Ruined.' He nodded, 'I threw it out.'

And studied his hand. Moist brown hand. She caught the sound of the river.

'Twenty pounds worth,' he added.

It was her turn, her duty, to repeat the apologies, assure him she would take care of the matter, but she wasn't able. In a lurch of unease, she remembered. The minute she saw him at the gate. A floundering which signalled, don't answer, whoever he is, let him go . . .

'Three days' work lost on top of that,' he came again. 'The chill stuck. Got at me in the end.'

She didn't reply nor did she look at him. Smoke lifted, curlicue, from her discarded cigarette.

'Look, I don't want you to think'—boldly now—'I don't want you to get the idea I'm taking advantage of you but, you see, it all adds up—doesn't it?'

She stared across.

'I can't afford to drop that much,' he said, 'If it was a smaller sum, I'—

'Stop.'

What she wanted to say now had to be thrust into the moil and confusion he'd loosed. And, helpless, she foresaw its effect.

'You've come for your money?'

At once, it stripped everything. The room was gone, there was the water rising, the elms, the hand, her flailing cries.

'Remember, it was your life I saved.'

She could see him plainly, the figure on the bank, negotiator.

'Your life, mind you.'

'My God,' she tore at him, 'that's it, my *life*.'

Hand withheld, keeping her there.

'How can I pay you for that? There's no paying for'—

'Hold on a'—

'How?'

'Look,' he said, a fresh approach, the veer, 'All right, I don't want much. Even a fiver.'

'No'—her lungs swamped.

'Right,' he said—leaning forward reasonably, 'Just a couple of quid?'

His nearness and some gross knowledge in his expression sickened her, reviving the ultimate scream, she moved back in the chair.

'Get out.'

He didn't move.

'You didn't say that the night I dragged you from the river.'

'Please go.'

'Skinflint,' he rose, 'I saved your stinking life.'

She heard him leave the room.

'Bitch,' he called from the porch.

The door banged.

She stayed there. After a while, she left to go upstairs. Half-way up, she heard a voice, bitter, her own, *Get out*. Then she went on up to have a bath.

Gunning's Word

We are dice in the hands of God The Gambler—there's not a doubt of it. Is any man safe? Look what happened to little Paul Pritchard: Paul made one slip, one solitary slip—and he'd had it. He went down to Neligan's this grand summer evening to arrange with Frank about the canopy-bearers for Thursday's procession, and who should be there but Gunning—

'Paul himself—fresh from Damascus,' Gunning opened, 'Name your poison, Paul.'

'Not now, Mick, thanks'—Paul shied towards the door— 'Just came in to'—

'What's seldom is wonderful, Paul'—advancing, Gunning swept him amiably forward and on to a stool by the counter— 'Now. Name your poison.'

'Bitter lemon,' said Paul.

'May it run through you'—Gunning grinned, and ordered a double-Irish for himself.

Gunning was the region's champion boozer. The curious thing was that he seemed to thrive on dissipation. True he'd yielded most of his innards to the surgeons, true he'd wrecked a good law practice, and true he'd driven the wife to an early old age. Gunning, however, was still there, in funds, and blooming. Everyone preached at him but it was pointless. The sermon concluded, Gunning—petting the immaculate handkerchief in the immaculate breast-pocket of the immaculate suit—would remark—

135

'Resilient class of an evening, don't you think?'

Gunning's favourite word: resilient.

Meanwhile, conversation was proceeding. Or, rather, Gunning was. Paul sat above the bitter lemon and listened to the usual tale of another evening on the batter. Gunning had gone into the city to a dog-meet, met so-and-so—a trainer, got a tenner on a tasty outsider, then off about midnight to the trainer's headquarters where they'd christened—as far as he could remember—a new-born bitch, best of breeding, with champagne, then retired to the trainer's house where there was a party going on, and—etc., etc., etc.

'Sounds like a great romp,' said Paul.

'It was a kind of a Tercentenary Waxies' Dargle, Paul'— Gunning gave the nod for another double—'A Tercentenary Waxies' Dargle.'

Paul said nothing.

'Well, and how're things with you, tell me,' Gunning enquired, 'Still piling up the shekels, I expect?'

'Mick,' Paul put down the bitter lemon, 'will you tell me something?'

'Of course.'

'Did it ever occur to you to kick the bottle out of your life?'

'Often, Paul, often—but, with the assistance of my good Guardian Angel, I was always able to put the'—

'For God's sake, Mick'—Paul seemed suddenly reduced to two brightly honed cheek-bones—'cut out the balderdash.'

And didn't he blitz Gunning. Disgrace to his home, to his profession, to the town, time he got some sense, a man of his age, but he'd listen to no one, all right, nobody else mattered, but if nothing else would stop him, you'd imagine he might have some regard for his own health, that last hospital session had been damn nearly *it*, the town, as a matter of fact, had given him up for dead, and what about the next trip, no man's health could stand that pace, his couldn't stand it, nor would it, and he, Paul, wasn't a bit afraid to say to his face what was being said all over—

'There's a coffin booked for you, Mick'—he jabbed a finger at Gunning, kept jabbing it, he'd worked himself into what, for Paul, was a hell of a state—'If you don't lay off, you've a year, maybe eighteen months—and don't say'—still jabbing—'don't say you weren't told.'

The barman was waiting for Gunning to come out with it—

'Resilient class of an evening, don't you think?'

—but it didn't come. Instead, Gunning studied Paul who, jabbing finger recalled to base, was catching his breath, and—

'I'll bury you, Paul,' said Gunning—his smile the smile of one who has been granted a rare illumination, 'I'll bury you, boy.'

Paul looked at him.

'I,' said Gunning, 'will—bury—you.'

Fair enough. It gave Paul a slight dunt at the time but—why make a fuss over a thing like that?—he put it out of his mind. And yet the next time he saw Gunning—it was on the street—he'd willingly have turned back or whipped over to the other footpath only, of course, it would have been bare-faced. Bracing himself, he kept going, just 'Nice day, Mick,' he wouldn't stop, lick by, and—

'Day, Mick.'

'Paul'—

Gunning's arm barred the way.

'Paul,' said Gunning—with a smile, 'I'll bury you.'

And moved on.

There you have the commencement exercises. They met, say, five times in the following three weeks. Each time, as it happened, there was company. And, each time, Gunning delivered his good-natured warning, loudly, so's all could hear—

'Paul, I'll bury you.'

'No bother to you, Mick.'

'No one I'd rather have do it'—

Paul carried it off fairly well but he felt that bringing the thing into the public arena was a bit much.

It was the wife, a few weeks later, who noticed him going into himself. Turning mopy. Especially in the evenings—

'What's wrong with you?'

'Nothing.'

'Something at that last meeting of The Knights?'

'What are you talking about?'

'Or is it the business?'

'Business was never better, thank God.'

'What's up with you, then?'

'Nothing.'

A day or two later, he told her. He'd come home from a Removal of Remains where, in spite of precautions, he'd bumped into Gunning, there'd been another—exchange, and . . . he told her the whole story.

'Well, you're all babies, I know,' the wife gazed on him in wonder, 'but this is the livin' limit.'

'I know,' said Paul, 'It's stupid. I know that.'

'And so this'—she hadn't taken her gaze off him—'is what you're mopy about?'

'I wouldn't mind if he hadn't made it public.'

'Shure what difference does'—

'I don't like being made a spectacle. By a sot.'

'But, dear, it's all in your own mind, don't'—

'It's not all in my own mind. I told you it's public.'

138

'Don't be worrying about it, just put the whole nonsense out of your head.'

It was about half-nine. She fixed up his jar, and put him to bed early—

'All you want to do is relax,' she told him, 'You work too hard anyway.'

Whereupon the wife does what wives always do. The very next day, didn't she pay a call on Maura Gunning, took her courage in her hands, and explained the whole thing, Mick obviously meant no harm but she was afraid it was getting in on Paul, she might be mistaken, the children were all away now, nest empty, and, no doubt, men also went through a change of life in their own peculiar fashion but, anyway, would Maura, if she could, drop a word, discreetly . . .

'To be sure, I will,' Maura was a good sort, 'He doesn't pay much heed to me but I'll see what can be done.'

That was Tuesday. Friday afternoon, Paul was flicking through invoices in the office at the rear of the shop when he heard steps, looked up, and there was Gunning—

'Well, Mick?'

Gunning, strangely solemn, hesitated in the doorway. He was wearing a black hat which Paul didn't recollect having seen on him before.

'What can I do for you?'

If Gunning had said what he usually said, Paul—on home ground—might conceivably have gone for him. But Gunning didn't.

'Paul,' he stepped into the office, 'you know that little—game—we've been playing?'

'Yes.'

'Listen,' Gunning looked earnestly at the floor, looked up, continued, 'It was only a game, Paul. In other words, when I said—what I said—I didn't mean it, Paul, you understand that?'

Paul, looking helplessly into Gunning's large grey eyes, might have nodded—he couldn't afterwards be sure.

'Shake,' said Gunning.

Paul stuck out a hand. It was taken in a powerful grip. Gunning left.

And, under a skin of sweat, Paul deduced instantly what had happened. He waited until the shop closed at six, and a further half-hour until the staff had gone. Then he went up-stairs, confronted the wife, and ballyragged her from attic to cellar. It was their first row in thirty years of marriage.

The moping continued but the wife didn't realise how serious the situation was until she opened a letter of his by mistake one morning a month later, and discovered a doctor's bill. Ten guineas—a consultation fee, and it was from a well-known heart man in the city. The date clicked. Paul had been to the city that day—business trip. She presented it to him at lunch—

'What, pray God, is this?'

He looked at it—'So?'

'Shure you have no heart trouble?'

'It was just a check.'

'A check? And you haven't lost a day in bed as long as I've known you?'

'I know that.'

'And he said your heart was fine?'

'That's right.'

She didn't pursue the matter but, that evening, she got him into the car, and they drove twenty miles to her cousin, a GP, and, incidentally, a first-class man. He examined Paul top to bottom, and gave his verdict. Not a thing wrong except nerves. Paul was, to put it simply, het-up—

'You've been too hard at it, Paul,' he told him, 'Rest far more. You're not an old man—but you're not a young man either. My advice to you is a month's holiday, two months' if you can spare it.'

'The heart *is* fine, Michael,' the wife asked, 'He was inclined to get'—

'The heart is fine—and will remain fine—so long as he relaxes. If he doesn't, I make no promises.'

'Thanks, Michael,' said Paul, and 'Thank you, dear,' he added as—looking neither left nor right—he led her towards the car.

The cousin could have told them, there and then, exactly how it would go—but he wasn't being paid for that. They took three weeks on the continent, a super-charged tour which fitted in Lourdes, Fatima, the Belgian shrine at what's-its-name, and four 'Great Cathedrals' for good measure. Paul came home fatigued and jittery, resumed work, took to drink-ing—upstairs cupboard drinking—and six months later was on the flat of his back with *angina*. He's on his feet again now but you wouldn't bet on his lasting. The general opinion is a year, eighteen months at the outside.

So there it is. Do he and Gunning ever meet? Frequently. Does Gunning ever say, well, what he used to say? Christ, no. On the contrary, he tells Paul that he's looking extraordinarily well. And, nothing if not humane, makes sombre references to another hospital trip which—doctor's insistence—he's got lined up for himself in the near future. In the bars, Gunning's judgement is that Paul 'lacked resilience'—

'He was never what you'd call a very resilient class of a man now, was he?' Gunning will enquire, raising his glass of the (undiluted) hard, 'I, certainly, would never have used that word of him.'

Naturally, the bars concur.

Imagine a Hare

Basking, backs to the front wall of the cottage, George, the old man, and Lois next on the window-sill. George lost no time in getting on to the hare—

'Guess what, Martin?' He looked at the old man abruptly, 'We got a hare the other day. Lois is doing it for dinner tomorrow.'

Tilting slightly, Lois hung—buttocks and hands—poised on the sill.

'Hare?' Martin asked, 'Hare did you say?'

'Yes,' spouse keeping her end up—just about, 'I'm going to cook hare-pie. It's'—steadying—'supposed to be great.'

Wiping his lips with the tattered blue handkerchief that lived in his fist, Martin watched the licheny flags strewn the opposite side of the yard.

'It's a real delicacy, Martin,' George risked—talking down was out but there was a lot at stake, 'Haven't you ever eaten hare?'

'To be sure I have'—quick there, bristled a bit maybe—'but, arrah, I wouldn't be bothered with it. No taste to it.'

Wilting, the visitors swopped grimaces.

'Tough as bog-oak the same hares,' Martin squinted into the sunlight, 'And rank somehow. On top of that, hang them for an hour, and they'd go musty if you didn't pray over them.'

'Now wait a minute, Martin'—George had been squaring

for a rally—'That was the hare *you* had. I had hare in Iowa once—it was the best meal I ever tasted.'

Iowa! Lois buried her eyes under blistered lids. Chuckling, Martin made for the gap—

'Iowa, is it?' He removed his hat, studied it, put it on again, 'Well, you bring one of your Iowa hares over here sometime and I'll give it a try—maybe. But'—he pointed, the direction vague, the disdain complete—'for those leathery codgers they have in this country, I tell you I wouldn't eat one if it was to be my last bite on this earth.'

And he thumped his stick on the cobbles.

The business had started two days ago when Bob Donegan, the painter—he was living twenty miles north—called by the house they'd rented in the town—

'On the mountains since morning,' he bawled out of waders and cartridge belts and the hunter's beaded glow—'Something for the pot'—tossing them the hare.

'A hare!' Agape. 'You're sure, Bob, I mean, won't Marilyn'—

'Four more out there,' he waved towards the car, 'It's all yours.'

Bob left, and the hare—dun length stiffening on the kitchen table, head and neck pocked red, long ears and switchy eyes quenched for good—took over. Instantly Lois had her cookbook out—they'd have broiled hare or boiled hare or fried hare or hare-pie . . . George, meanwhile, circling the table, phrases from Yeats flying at him like caressing shrapnel, the lino and the walls sprouting heather, the cantankerous cistern upstairs a chatty mountain stream—

'Herbs,' Lois cried, flicking pages, 'Now George—Bayleaf? Garlic? Water-cress? Ooohps'—

'Oh'—

144

They bumped—laughing, hugged, parted. The hare. Wild odours coursed the kitchen—

'We'll have wine, Lois'—George, from his resumed circling —'A good ripe Burgundy, say'—he looked round—'Lois?'

Lois was racing out next door to Mrs. Keenan who would be, and was, making her daily devotions to the brass knocker.

'Know what?' she rushed up, the neighbour turning at the commotion, 'We've just been given a hare. Shot on the mountains today. And I'm going to do a marvellous meal'—

'Hare?' Mrs. Keenan vibrated chastisement, 'That for a story—God, girl, I thought you won The Sweep.'

'But hare's wonderful,' Lois stood her ground, 'It's a beautiful dish'—

'Doctors differ'—dropping a rag into the biscuit tin on the steps, selecting another, back to the work—'I wouldn't touch it if you paid me. And if I presented it to The Boss in there, he'd throw it out the window, me with it.'

'But why?'

Mrs. Keenan puckered, paused, at length gave judgement —'Ah, they do be old, you know, hares.'

'They can't all be old,' Lois pinned her, 'Besides, this is a young hare. You can tell'—

'They're tough though, girl,' belting hell out of the knocker, 'tough to the heels.'

'But it's a young hare, it couldn't possibly be'—

'They're all young until you take a knife and fork to them,' Mrs. K., small as she was, spoke from an almighty height, 'Still, I suppose if you're bent on cooking it, the divil won't stop you.'

'You bet I'll cook it,' Lois retreated, rumping defiance, 'And you'll come in and sample it, what's more.'

A minor repulse—and anyway, as George said, Mrs. Keenan's aspirations related much more to The Scapular of

The Sacred Heart then *Le Cordon Bleu*. Yet, when they breezed out for a walk that evening, they were—in a way—prepared for what happened. Excitedly, they told half-a-dozen acquaintances, including even the schoolmaster, Frank Mc Inerney, and the wife—two who might be expected to know the difference. Everyone listened—politely. And everyone dismissed. Hare? Hare was the poor man's rabbit. Fit for tinkers, possibly, in hard times. But what was wrong with hare? Rigmarole denigration of the hare. Examine the criticism, and it came to nothing. But examination was out—with hares—and obstinacy was in. The negative chorus soured their nights sleep. With the postman next morning, George—smelling of defeat—was foolish enough to raise the subject. The postman, fluently echoing and enlarging all previous calumnies, wiped the floor with him.

The inquest was querulous.

'Lack of imaginative response,' George defined.

'And they're supposed to have imagination?'—Lois.

'That, dear, is the line.'

'Clods'—

The calm hand on high but fretfully, 'Don't let'—

'They've taken the whole good out of it. I don't know if I can even cook it myself now.'

'We'll cook it,' George banged the table.

It was fortuitous, in the circumstances, that they'd arranged to drive out and see old Martin the next day. The town, they both knew, was one thing, the hills another. And Martin had more life in him than the Keenans, the McInerneys, and the whole urban tribe put together.

'No. Wouldn't look the side of it,' Martin reiterated, 'Not if you threw me a sovereign for every mouthful I chanced.'

Et tu, Martin—and good-bye to the hare. Followed three

146

seconds silence, all present standing, as a mark of—irritation mostly. And the goblin jumped into George's mouth—

'But this is a special hare, Martin'—skip one beat—'There's a strange story to it.'

'How so?'

'Well, the way we caught him'—rippling here from the tentative to the jocose, and back again: checking, Lois' amused stare, the sharp lift to the old man's ear: proceeding—'The way he turned up, you know.'

'What way was that now?'

And, go on or go back, George? didn't arise. Metering a collusive tremor from Lois, he was away ahead of himself—shifting to face his audience as, out of the air, promise-crammed, the story flowed—

'Let's see'—scratch the poll, good—'Yes, Lois was out in the yard, hanging clothes or whatever on Wednesday—it was about three o'clock, about three, Lois, was it?'

'Three to three-thirty'—Lois chiming as if she'd had six weeks' rehearsal—'bout that.'

'When'—George centre-stage now, getting the feel of his script—'the hare bursts through the hedge at the bottom of the garden, stops, looks left, looks right'—the miming simple but stylish—'and belts straight up the path, fifty an hour.'

'What'd ye do?'

'The funny thing was'—taking Martin's scrutiny open-armed—'we hadn't to do a thing.'

'Nothing'—Lois again on cue—'Nothing. At. All.'

'Well, then?' Looking from one to the other, 'How'd it go?'

'He streaked up the path, stopped dead'—supplying the streak, the halt—'and'—rising from his hunkers, George delivered it, throwaway—'jumped right into Lois' arms.'

They watched Martin. Waited.

'So you held on?' he turned to Lois.

'Tight'—Lois uncertain, recovering—'Surprised as he was, Martin, but I held. Then'—pass the buck, quick—'I shouted, screamed'—

'And you came?'

'Ran out,' for George, gaily, the *coup de grace*—'got hold of him, and broke his neck. Just like that.'

Again they watched him, waited, certain that he'd—

'I'll tell you where that hare came from'—he was hobbling out for a better view—'The cliffs there'—stick stiffly pointing seaward to the uneven cobalt line miles away—'They're hunting hares up there night and day. That hare, I'm going to tell you, was on the run.'

'From the cliffs he came'—vehement—'and on the run.'

'You—think so, Martin?'

'Down the length of the cliffs'—his back to them, already mapping the route—'across Moymore, over Corlurgan Bog, up The Back Road, cleared the bit of a river, chased along behind the houses'—stick tracing helter-skelter—'panicked at something or other, cut through the fence into the garden, didn't know where he was—and was captured easy.'

George usurped—was edging back to the wall. The zigzag shadow on the ground stilled, Lois opened her mouth to say something—didn't. Martin's stance there was—a seething.

'Listen,' he turned to face—to command—them, 'I'll tell you exactly where that chase started. Listen now.'

Under the yellowy stubble, you could spot the slack cheeks' fire, above that roamer glances catching the blaze—

'You know that coomb this side of Hag's Head, a hive of hares from the beginning of time, the same now, and ever will be. Right'—he pointed, two yards away, taut in discovery—'There's your hare in a basket of ferns, sunning himself nicely and dreaming his dinner when'—the stick walloped a stone in

reach—'Christ of a sudden up with the ears, the hind legs
a tremble, and the beagles in spate at the northern end'—he
paused to let them hear that: and it came, atonal, drifting, the
far undulant yapping of the hounds—'Now'—imperious,
pulling them back, the hare—'First he's a ball, nothing in his
head but The Prayers For The Dying'—cowering, blessing
himself—'until'—unleashing—'kick of the hind boys, the
pack a hundred yards off, he flattens the ears, stretches
his length, and we're away, man'—he squealed delight
—'pepperin' the wind.'

It careered on from there, the whole countryside poured
into the yard, every inch of the chase: men, beagles, the brown
flying blur—twist and feint, ditch, stream, meadow-grass,
rushes. The floor of the yard bucked like a ship assailed, ducks
and hens scattered, the pony screeched in the field below the
house, Lois clutched the sill, George hugged the wall, and the
old man, hoarse, flushed, vulnerable as a child—or a hare,
flailed his shadows on . . . the hare, the hare—

'I cut right at the first dip where the yapping behind me has
no eyes—and I sink in the bracken'—at his feet a patch of
bracken stirred, minutely, resumed its station—'I have to
have breath, the lungs in ribbons, I lie there'—straining for
breath—'Bees foostering above me. Bog-cotton going up like
flag-poles. The beagles away to the right, loud but when
they're barking they're not biting. Listen'—weed and stone
listened—'There's a brindled bastard in that pack would
smell swallows flying south in pitch night. Listen. Look at
him. Black snout up. Shouldering out to the fringe. Look . . .'

And they were looking, to where a stone wall—chippings of
light brilliant in the interstices—contained the yard, looking
with him, waiting, fugitive, for the brindled hound, snout up,
shouldering at the fringe . . . of the white afternoon . . .

Even from Martin, they'd never heard anything like it—but, or course, it was all wrong. Nothing to do, however, but sit it out, and soon as it was over—clatter of the stick, the revels ended—George was groping for a chance to explain, make amends—

'That was great, Martin,' he began bravely, 'And you know'—

'A drink's what's needed,' Martin proclaimed, his exhiliration beyond compliments, 'I'll root out a few bottles of stout.' He tramped inside, gusts of the chase still clinging to him.

The yard rested.

'Well,' George clawed at his beard, 'How do we get out of this, dear?'

For answer, Lois gave him the bleakest gesture in her repertoire—the midriff shrug.

The lull while they drank from stained mugs gave him plenty of time to frizzle. The talk—politics now, Martin ebullient—allowed no opportunity to set the thing right. Subdued, Lois hung there. Several times, he thought, oh, let it go, what the hell? but the yard, still reverberating, jagging, wouldn't let him drop the thing. Yet, yard or no, Martin's garrulity—on the subject of German spies in Ireland during the war, for God's sake—did eventually free him, bestowing, at the same time, a sort of ease. It was everybody's misfortune that half-an-hour later, they were about to leave, Martin himself—no warning—skipped back to the chase, and again, pernickety *revenant*, the affair was clamouring that amends be made—

'That hare now, I'm thinking. Supposing he didn't come from the cliffs at all'—inside him, they could hear a new drumming, multiplying hypotheses, elaborations, by-ways: pushing up the hat's brim, he leaned on the gatepost, and viewed a spread of valleys thrusting inland, 'Supposing for a minute'—

'But Martin'—and George had lunged: the chance here—
he could see it—with the balm of a joke besides—'We're certain he came from the cliffs.'

'Certain?'

'Yes—we know he did.'

'How so?'

'Well'—George's tone, light and airy, gathered a thin
determination—'You know when Lois was holding the hare in
the yard that time, something odd happened.'

'What happened?'

'Well'—he heard Lois snap her bag shut—and interpreted
—but he had to go on now—'The hare, you see'—looking
Martin half in the eye, smiling, asking for tolerance—'the
hare—mentioned it to Lois. That he'd come from the cliffs.'

Hare-pie was marvellous, Lois assured Bob Donegan, when,
next time round, he enquired how she'd enjoyed the hare.

'You, George?' he tried.

'Loved it,' George said, looking up from his book, and
seeing—for the hundredth time—those veins of doubt clot
and darken in the old man's tethered eyes.

Fable

Eileen: frail, small face, tight blue eyes, and a head, unwashed, of grey stringy hair. With her sister, she worked in the house of the town's biggest merchant. When the sister took sick and died, she was badly shaken.

'Give her a year,' Miko Carroll said the day of the funeral, 'and you can put her under.'

'Six months,' Dan Murtagh contradicted, 'If that. She's whipped.'

What did happen was that she turned odd, slept by day, lived by night—if you wanted to call it 'living.' Often she could be heard going to the well about midnight, a sing-song jumble fighting the noise of her clattering bucket. Occasionally, she went back to her old job for a day but she was altered. Competent and contented before, she moped now or worked idly, she was cross, needed fussing all the time.

She hadn't been seen for a month when she strayed in for work this morning. About eleven o'clock the son of the house happened to come down from the shop. In the kitchen he found his mother, the two young housemaids, and Eileen. He was a good-natured joker, and, catching sight of Eileen, he quipped—

'Isn't it a wonder you wouldn't get yourself a man, Eileen, for the company? There's Andy Logan, they say he's cracked on you.'

All watched. She was crouched for the stove's heat.

'I did without them this long'—turning she faced him—
'And I'll last it now.'

Snapping her duster, she streeled out and away to some
corner.

'You shouldn't be at her like that,' the mother chastized.

But the son smiled, the maids smiled, and she had to smile
too.

Logan—that crabbed eccentric who'd never had truck with
women. And Eileen. From that hour the names were coupled.
Eileen Lynch and Andy Logan.

Irregularly, Eileen still came to work. Whenever she did,
the house played the game. The maids most of all, two
scattered pieces from the back streets. Looking up from the
sweeping of a floor, one would begin—'Oh, Eileen, I nearly
forgot. There was a message from Logan. He'll be out to you
tonight.' Or dropping the item with a cobweb dislodged from
the ceiling—'He was in the town last week, Eileen. They're
saying he has nothing on his mind but you.' Eileen would only
scowl, and stamp off about her doubtful chores.

One afternoon the mistress entered the kitchen to discover
her hooped over the big table in a whirl of scrubbing. She
watched the spindly arm move back and forth, brush spewing
water and suds over the broad surface. And, from habit, threw
her some talk of Logan—

'Seriously now, Eileen, would you not give Andy a thought?'

The scrubbing slopped to a pause.

'What would Andy Logan want with me?' Steeped in steam
and suds, Eileen didn't raise her head, 'Me, is it—the heel of
an old stocking getting worse every day?'

The spindle wrist rushed to a frenzy of scrubbing, the bent
body shrank into itself, water sloshed needlessly. And, intrigued, the mistress departed.

The news staggered the place but, putting her on trial, they sensed belief in the shy welcome she gave their taunts. Then someone remembered that she'd been appearing more regularly of late, seemed to be coming out of herself. They put her on trial further. Oh, there was no doubt of it, unburdened hours followed his name. Logan the lover, Eileen beloved—shop, storeroom, kitchen and pantry, hailed the union.

The yarn had, extraordinarily, worked the chance miracle —made her hard-working and bearable. That was one good reason for keeping it alive. But, in any case, it was too sweet to part with. There was clownery to convulse you in the antics of the old one. If she happened to be in bad form, someone would be given orders to deliver the latest word.

'The Boss met him on the road, Eileen. He'll be out to you on Sunday.'

'He said that?'

'He did.'

'Sunday?'

'Sunday—and you make sure to be there.'

No more to it then but watching the life flow back into her, taking away years until you were left with a girl awake to any (even the most oblique) reference to her lover, and thrilling frequently to references which did not involve him at all.

That the lover never came on Sunday, never came at any time was irrelevant.

'Well, was he up to see you yesterday?'

'Yesterday? In that drizzle? The man has more wit.'

The bite in her answer put a stop to prying. It was hot or it was cold, it was blustery or it was dull. He would come in his chosen time. She could wait.

The town got hold of the story, and joined in, colouring, expanding. Wedding bells for Eileen. Would she be married in white? There goes the bride! Constantly, jokers were halting her on the street—

'Eileen, what's this about you and Logan? Is it true he has the ring?'

She was well able for them.

'If he has, it's his affair'—lean face fronting them angrily—'And no business of yours.'

Afterwards, to the mistress, she would speak her fury at this meddling. Soothing, the mistress would agree: Eileen's personal life was her own concern.

So it was—until one morning the mistress wandered into the living-room to find her chatting a mirror as she cleaned it.

'Andy, I don't know'—she worked a fly-blown corner—'We have little sense at our age'—puzzled, rubbing spittle into the speckled surface—'I often hear them laughing . . . still . . .' Under her rambling duster the dull silver brightened. She stopped polishing, seemed to drown in the depths of glass: slowly, the rag began to move again, revolving, working lazily around the face which looked out, gums visible in a strange smile.

'Eileen'—

She spun from the mirror. The mistress—a bad night, some annoyance?—levelled her with a look.

'Eileen, you'll have to quit that game now. You know it was no more than a joke, that the man never heard of you, that'—

'A joke?' Eileen advanced, and her voice thrashed, *'Can't you leave us be?'*

The mistress shied, turned away, left her. An hour later Eileen appeared to have forgotten the scene but, in the house, it signalled a change. Not a sudden change but the slow toil of some venom in the air. The maids, for example, lost their zest in teasing, shut up altogether for a while, and, when they

resumed, found themselves harbingers not of joy but of
defeat—

'No news, Eileen? Talk of another woman, I hear . . . Is
Logan in the country at all?'

She dismissed them as a pair of schemers.

The shop-boys caught on, saw the possibilities, and joined
enthusiastically in this new game. Logan's made his will, the
youngest suggested, all's left to The Missions. The message
was dispatched to the kitchen.

Quickly, this approach was established, operating not with
the old freedom but with an energy that compensated. You
saw Eileen. You picked at her. Logan's treachery. Peculiarly
though, the more he was defamed, the greater her belief. Her
easy stride said, I love, am beloved. There was no getting past
that.

Of course—since she'd decided to be stubborn—the thing
spread, and grew in vehemence. On a large cement wall along
her road out of town was chalked the message—'Andy Logan
and Maggie Foyle.' (Maggie was the town's 'natural', and
bearing nameless children long as she'd been able.) The
skittish girls from the cottages near shouted to her the full
night they'd had with Andy—they couldn't wait to be in his
warm clutch again. And packs of children sometimes beagled
her home, tonguing their 'Good night'—'Andy Logan doesn't
want her, Andy Logan doesn't want her . . .'

Still, she was not disturbed: in her, at all times, that ridic-
ulous ease, as if she knew—beyond confusion—that her path
was to the aisle.

Once she did show fear.

A few of the boys got the notion of visiting her and bringing
a 'Logan' along. The oldest of the bunch—grizzled face,
sulky gob, cramp in the bones—could play the part. Inside,

and settled, he would be blunt, tell her he'd have no more of it, that all was over. And then? That was the point of the expedition.

About ten o'clock one Sunday night they arrived at her door. The spokesman, postboy on that road, knocked adventurously. No answer. He knocked again. The door opened. Hand on the latch, she stared out—

'Well, Michael?'

'Eileen,' he propped himself against the jamb to set her at ease, 'It's only that Andy was going by'—thumbing back at the others, glancing round to beckon—'and he had a wish to come in and see you.'

He stood aside. Hustled to the threshold, 'Andy' made to enter.

'*Go away.*'

The door banged. That was all she said but they could hear the small sounds of her terror within. For a minute or two they stood outside, feeling as if they'd threatened her life. Then they strolled back to the town, wondering, got drunk, and told the story afterwards—still wondering.

Next morning, Eileen was singing as before. The tussle went on. She held to her lover. Since she wouldn't yield, there was nothing to do eventually except suffer her.

.

Logan died off.

'Bad news, Eileen,' the mistress broke it, 'they say Andy's dead.'

She expected Eileen to deny it, flitter her where she stood but, coldly, she took the words, went ahead with her work. When they looked round again, however, she was gone.

At the burial, the main interest was not in Logan but in Eileen. Would she appear—weeping and widowy at the foot of the grave? Crumple as the first clay drummed? Chafe her eyes red as they patted earth smooth above him? It would be a poor funeral without her.

They waited that day, in hope, but Eileen didn't come.

Her absence was soon explained. She'd gone odd again, was jailed in the cottage. The death, as might have been expected, had wrecked her. She was much in people's minds now. Her future you could surmise: a few years among pots and ashes, then The County Home—to dribble out her days. There was a move to have the local charitable organizations supply her with necessities.

The forecast of her future was, in the main, correct. She didn't exactly starve to death nor did she freeze to death but it was that kind of decline. She forgot all about Logan, the palpitations, the fever of love, the fidelity which couldn't be undermined. Most people forgot about it. In the cemetery the day she was buried, Miko Carroll remarked to Dan Murtagh—

'Remember the fun we had with her about Logan?'

The diggers were tidying, the crowd already moving off.

'Logan?' said Murtagh, 'Fun about Logan?'

Carroll was about to explain when Dermot Dillon came across to see if they were game for Mullingar, the races, next week. And somehow the Logan business didn't come up again.

Wood Crumbles

When Father O'Donnell first came to the town, he was about fifty. Though turning a little towards flesh, he had a rangy clean-timbered build and a still supple stride. In dress he was neat but it was an irksome neatness and never elegance, as if the body chafed under it. His grey head of hair was boyishly trim, the face below it squarely set, edged with bony lines, and always shaven smooth. It was his housekeeper, one Margaret McKenna—a garrulous claw-hammer of a woman whom he'd recruited locally—who noised the matter of his obsession. Noticed it straight off, said Margaret—

'Margaret, you will see that the water is hot this evening?'

'To be sure, Father . . . Is it today you have your bath?'

'I have a bath every day, Margaret. You must see to it that the water is hot every day.'

'To be sure, Father . . .'

A bath every day: she swore it couldn't be healthy. She told the town, and the town was pleased. They could ponder the item for some time. Meanwhile, she saw to it that the water *was* hot, and each day he washed himself clean. The fifteen minutes before his evening meal were set aside for the task. At a quarter past six you could hear in the kitchen the rude gush of water into the bath, and at six-thirty the pipy croak of it rushing away.

The bath, it must be said, was only one charge. There were others which Margaret quickly listed. So far as she could see, his hands were always clean but he washed them so often you'd wonder they didn't wear away. In the matter of personal linen he was insatiable: umpteen sets of everything continually ready, fresh and aired. (He might or might not desire a change but the snowy pile must be there in the hot-press.) About his bed-linen he was just as finicky, worse, indeed . . .

'Margaret, please change those sheets today.'

'The sheets on *your* bed, Father?'

'Yes, Margaret.'

'But, Father, they only went on the day before'—

'Margaret, they are not clean. Change them today.'

'To be sure, Father.'

'It's a Turkish-bath he'll be wanting next,' she complained to the gardener, and again swore it couldn't be natural.

The gardener didn't give her much heed but odd snippets kept turning up which tended to support her extreme views. Andy Flanagan—the Surveyor—reported meeting His Reverence by the lake one evening. Talk was proceeding harmlessly between them when—

'Look,' the priest interrupted, and the white hand gestured.

Andy looked towards the lake.

A pair of swallows were skimming the water—down the lake in reckless flight, wheeling smoothly, returning on their course, angling down to splash themselves in the play of ripples, rising refreshed to curve away again—

'Do you notice it?' he enquired—eyes still flying with the swallows, 'Even with the birds—the need to keep clean.'

Against that, there were those who saw nothing unhealthy in the business at all. The man, as they put it, had a thing about keeping himself clean. Well, what if he had? It was remembered that the last parish priest had been assailed for his interest in cattle-breeding. And his predecessor—an authority on the scriptures—had been accused of being 'cracked on the books.' Now, a man was being attacked for keeping himself clean. The next arrival, no doubt, would be whipped for saying his prayers. When he bought the lead coffin, however, even these people stopped to think again.

He'd been in the town about six months when it arrived on the midday train from the city one day, and for a couple of hours lay spectacularly on the platform, a long grey tightly-lidded box. Children never neglect such gifts. To a summons of instinct they appeared, and a tranced group encircled 'the thing'—defying the porter who several times ordered them home. At first, a cage of silence held the lot. Next, in the way of children, they pressed nearer, became familiar. At a closer view the naked 'coffinness' of it made impact. The momentary awe which resulted capsized to irreverence. Some dared to romp around it chanting a childish rhyme about funerals, burials, and worms.

A macabre sight: the fagged little station with its blowzy hoardings and musty platform, the spitting eyes of the porter from the office window, the weird vivacity of the children around the coffin, the gay choiring—

> *The worms crawl in*
> *And the worms crawl out,*
> *They go in thin*
> *And they come out stout . . .*

The appearance of a van, containing the priest's gardener and three other helpers, scattered the romp. After much exertion the coffin was loaded. The gardener went over to the office, signed a receipt, eyed the porter dumb, and drove away. The van trundled the half-mile to the town, through the main street as mundanely innocent as if it held a cargo of cabbage, and, to the whinge of gears, worked up the slope to The Parochial House.

They found the priest waiting jumpily. As they opened the van, he stood by. He looked, came forward wordlessly, and laid his hand on the solid coldness of the lead. The men shifted back, stood there clumsily.

'It's a very nice job, Father'—the gardener.

The priest remained with his eyes stuck on the coffin, that hand still caressing the unresponsive lead.

'Will you take it inside, please?'

Manoeuvring the van, struggling with steps, battling with angles of the threshold, they dragged it into the porch.

'If you could leave it in that room—to the left there?'

They forced it into a room off the hall. From a distance, Margaret, busy about some convenient chore, watched 'the new lodger' (as she afterwards named it) moving in.

The chosen room was bare of furniture, unused till now, a bleak raw-cold room which never saw the sun. They juggled the coffin to the centre of the floor. It lay there—and, strangely, the room was complete. The room owned the coffin, and the coffin owned the room. You felt they had been waiting for each other.

'Thank you.'

The men withdrew, and went off. Margaret slipped below to her kitchen. When she rambled upstairs again, an hour later, the priest was standing in the doorway of the room. He was looking in at the lead coffin, and—easy to tell—he was taking great ease from it. Looked as if he could stay there forever. Still, she noted, he did not forget to wash himself that evening at the regular hour.

Opinions now ran wild as weeds. A few saw in it proof of his holiness: he desired to have near him this reminder of his last end, they said, the coffin (forever by him while he lived) would be an emblem of his destiny. More saw in it the reverse

—an unpriestly love of luxury: he was making certain of a
burial in style by buying a lead coffin in advance at the expense
of the parish. There were others who at once linked it with
his 'need to keep clean'. However, when they looked more
closely here, the conclusions seemed so utterly gross that they
let the upturned stone fall back into place, stepped away
from it, and remained silent.

They didn't remain so for long because they found a voice.
Margaret's. She had no doubts at all, and she was not a woman
to bury her thoughts—

'It's the worms,' she announced, 'He's in dread of the worms.
He'll not have them fatten on his body, and the lead's for to
hold them out. He's in livin' terror of the worms.'

People were shocked.

'Have wit, woman,' she was told, 'that's no talk to be going
on with.'

Yet say it she did, frequently, and not without gaining
ground. Surprisingly soon, it wasn't unusual to find this or
that solid-minded citizen asserting that the coffin *was* all part
of something sickly, and that when it had gone this far, well,
who could tell what his next prank might be?

Meanwhile, 'the new lodger' was settling in. Nor was it
neglected. Margaret reported that the priest was habitually
glancing into the room where the coffin waited. To make sure, it
appeared, that the guest was comfortable. He also had a trick
of leaving the door of that room ajar—to establish, or feign,
some kind of communication. And then he started displaying
it to his visitors.

Dozens had this experience. From the tidiness of the celibate
sitting-room he would capriciously jerk his caller—

'Something I want to show you . . . This way, please . . . I'd
like you to see it.'

Down the hall, and into 'the room.' You may imagine the

caller's plight, faced with the shrinal absurdity of it, and, at the same time, flayed with an awareness of all that had been said, half said, or left unsaid on the subject. Lost to that panic, the priest would allow the lead to dazzle him awhile before rescuing the moment with a comment which never altered—

'Wood crumbles, it's true,' he would say earnestly, 'but you can depend on lead.'

There was release in the remark, and, on the surge of it, the safety of the sitting-room might be regained.

Did the presence of the coffin give him ease? Many people marked the calm which came over him when admiring or even talking of it and yet, coffin or no, there was still this ceaseless washing, this passion for snowy linen, this abrupt disrobing in conversation. One item which bared the root-fast grip of his need was its repeated intrusion in the Sunday sermons. In the midst of a talk on, say, 'Respect for The Sabbath,' he would suddenly urge—'And look to it that you keep yourselves clean, for the clean are the beloved of God.' Or again, in a sermon on 'Honesty in Trade,' he would warn —'Always, my dear brethren, see to it that you do the clean thing . . .' At such moments the congregation would quiver as if struck in the mouth. And such moments were not forgotten.

The years of his ministry crept away like altar-boys who'd served their term. There were no further sensations, no additional lodgers were received in The Parochial House. He died, after an illness of a few months, at the age of seventy-two. During the last months what possessed him was the coffin. The stories of the house-keeper, nurse, doctor, and the the odd visitors all tallied on this. Repetitively, he would force promises that he or she would not fail him, would see him buried in the coffin below. Vexingly and endlessly, he would ask the nurse (or whoever was present) to slip down-stairs and see if it was still safely there. In answering this request there was no chance of pretence because he would listen through the bedroom door for the soothing steps of the messenger, going—five across the landing, fourteen on the stairs, six down the hall—and returning. And to the martyred 'Yes' of the messenger he always gave the same answer, the same unalterable phrase—

'Wood crumbles, it's true, but you can depend on lead.'

He died, and was waked.

The day when he must be coffined came.

They carried the corpse downstairs to place it in the coffin. In the room off the hall the heavy lid, removed in advance, lay on the floor beside it. With reverent hands they lowered the body—and discovered the mistake. It was only two inches but those two inches were everything.

The stiffness of death will not yield nor will lead. There was only one thing to do. A saw cut through the lead. A fresh wooden end was fitted in haste. And, in that blemished coffin, they buried him.

An Aspect of the Rising

Opposite Adam and Eve's, the up-river east wind that would frizzle a mermaid's fins a zephyr tickle the second I sighted her. Plump chiaroscuro: black bobbed hair, white cheeks, black coat, white calves, black shoes, high-heeling along the far footpath. She looked recklessly like herself, in her wisdom gazed neither to the left nor to the right but let the plastic bag winking on her rump com'ither me through the scooting traffic and urgent to her side.

'We're in business'—I matched her step, leaned towards her, eager as a guitar.

'Fast from the trap, aren't you'—she spoke from the lips out, never slackened pace—'Wonder you weren't made ointment of crossing the street.'

'You're beautiful'—pursuing, I ladled compliments into her small skintight ear, and now she coy'd. The black pencilled line above her visible eye, the right, took my admiration. Oblique but eloquent of the horizontal, a masterpiece. Still we hurried—

'Where're we going?'

'You have a car?'

Had a car.

'I have to have a cup of coffee'—her mauve mouth belonged to the first woman, the destined rib—'You can get the car. And wait for me up here outside The Last Post.'

She went. Captive, I watched her buttocks acclaim a royal

leaving. Her scent stayed. A firm scent. And ready. Appled. That was it. Apples and muscles. Taffeta flashing above her bright-bare calves, the door of The Last Post opened before her.

Philomena, she introduced herself. And my instinct, I decided, had been sound. Anything with ears on it bar a pot is the rule along the river most nights but here was a real professional, her every motion *credo*—

'How're they hanging?' she enquired as we drove off towards Kingsbridge and The Park beyond.

'Two eggs in a hanky.'

Chuckling, she produced cigarettes, lit two, and passed one to me. They were Polish and smuggled—a sailor from Riga.

'Poles, I say to him,' she reminisced, settling back in the seat—knees sudden and vocal as the skirt rose, 'poles is right.'

Sure of your wares is sure of your stares. Philomena, slowly, fingered open her coat, and—I glanced across—the wares, big unbiddable breasts, trim belly, and roomy thighs, began to move and converse under blouse and skirt as if equally sure of themselves. To the silencer in these excitements I bowed. She, reading me with black eyes, understood, and, leaning over, petted my abundant crotch. Jesus, I thought—giddy— I'll have to be dug out of her. The last buses were being shunted home, on the roof of The Brewery a bouncy moon. Apples and the contraband of The Baltic odorous about us, we took the hill, sped through the gates and into The Park.

'Here, Philomena?'

A few hundred yards in, and impetuous, I was steering for a convenient nest under the adjacent and glooming trees.

'No, keep going. Right. Keep going. There's a little spot I know. I'll show you the way'—

167

Venue. Between friends, I asked, what was the difference, here or there? No good. We drove. Insistent, she directed me, her neat coaxing hand slipping in and out of the light—'It's a special spot I have. Not far'—

On reflection, I yielded. She was right. Not any hole in the wall but a sanctified lair. What a woman! We passed The Zoo. A lion raged within, and down to our right flamingos fluttered and gossiped in the pink insomnia of their watery beds.

'The Zoo's grand,' she voiced dreamily, 'Keep going.'

Open spaces, right, left, this fork now, trees, silver choppy in the branches, no trees, silver seamless along the grass. Delay's a randy foreman. I glimpsed the dank remains of turfstacks which had warmed Dublin winters ago, I glimpsed the long-legged ghosts of slaughtered deer but I thought neither of the huddled fire nor the red jittery stag. She sat there, relaxed, substantial in the run of shadows, now and then nibbling my neck.

'Nearly there.'

'Christ,' I grouched, 'we'll be at The Boyne before we know it.'

Next moment—'Here,' she pointed, 'left'—

And (it wasn't just the voice, curiously level) I felt—alteration. On the turn, I inspected her. Sure enough, she was tight in the seat, tight as Christy's britches. Suspicion cranked me. No, I calmed myself. The cramp of an instant. It means nothing. We were driving towards a stand of fir and pine a hundred yards away, a large building visible in fragmented outline beyond. Deep into the trees, I pulled up. Philomena, my new Philomena, was out of the car, wordless, before I'd switched off the ignition. Worried, I followed.

Smell of the trees. And the place's seasoned privacy. And the midnight dusk. There she was—a stranger and grim—her back to a young fir a few yards off. What was she at? Climbing the palisade of her remove, I advanced. Rhinestones flickered but didn't beckon. I was beside her, whispering. Weep for my whispers. She was wood against that tree. My fingers implored. Colder than wood—

'What's wrong?'

Two bleak eyes, she stood there. I made a rude remark. It passed lightly through her—your hand through a ghost.

'What is it?' I tried again, 'What's wrong?'

Useless. I scanned her face, a hunter's face, stalking what? Wind skidded on the branches. Philomena and I waited. For five stinging seconds, and then the spurs of a mean anger raked me. Let me omit the vituperation I flung upon her. It shames my balls, and it balls my shame. Tranced black and white in a shaft of the moon, she paid, thank God, no heed. I wheeled to depart, and not three steps had I taken when the woman, catspitting, was soaring to her singular and sainted glory—

'You crawthumpin' get of a Spaniard that never was seen' —incredulous, I stopped: the wood rang—'with your long features and your long memory and your two and twenty-two strings to your bow, what crooked eggs without yolks are you hatching between Rosaries tonight?'

Birds racketing. The Spaniard? To a skelp of joy, I connected. The building beyond—Arus an Uactharain, De Valera himself under sharp and sharpening fire—

'Diagrams,' I heard, 'diagrams'—and a sneer bisected the word as it flew—'more of them you're amusing yourself with maybe, proving that A is B and B is C and a Republic is Jazus knows what until Euclid himself 'd be cracked in Dundrum trying to make y'out. But Professor Isosceles'—she drew harsh breath, raced on, discovering the beat of her scorn— 'it was damn all diagrams or anything else we got from you above in Boland's Mills when Simon Donnelly had to take over the command, you sitting there with your heart in your gob and your arse in a sling'—

Listen to me. There are sights you never forget. Her face wild, throat wilder, hands two kicking lanterns, knees ivory below—immobile and smooth, Philomena roasted The Long Fellow. Practice graced her, rancours unnameable and a fury of the bones powered her—she left nothing out, there was nothing she didn't fit in: The Treaty, The Civil War, The Oath, The Hangings of the 40's, Emigration, Inflation, Taxation, The Language, the lot. An eighth of a mile away, brooding or at his prayers, His Excellency heard not a word but, chosen by The Gods, I heard, the ground heard and the wind and the sky's cupped ear. We listened to that alto scurrility leap the air, listened in ecstasy and heard—reaches distant—backlane and gutter answer, stir, shift, and jig maddened to an old, a blithe, a bitter tune—

'You,' she cried aloud and aloft, 'you long spear in the side of a Christian people, May God drop a clog on you, May the Divil make a knot of you, May coals scorch you and may cinders choke you, May smoke annoy you and may soot destroy you, May the day peel your skins and the night screech your sins, May . . .'

Don't ask me how long it lasted but bring back Moses and I'll say it to his teeth: she finished that diatribe a creature of flame. You'd kneel to her—

'You there,' says she—there was barely a pause—into the shriven quiet, 'Are you comin' or goin'?'

I was dazzled but comin'. Gaily she murmured me in. Zips purred. The undergrowth lured. To it we went, and at it we stayed.

Birds settled again on the branches. In the great house beyond the trees—lights burning here and there, in the city below, and all over Ireland, medals were being dusted, ribbons spruced, orations polished and artillery oiled for The Fiftieth Anniversary of The Insurrection.